# The Suspects

**Mabel and Violet Mysteries, Volume 4**

Joan Havelange

Published by Brown Wolf Publishing, 2025.

# Also by Joan Havelange

**Mabel and Violet Mysteries**
Wayward Shot
Death and Denial
The Trouble with Funerals
The Suspects

*"Mabel and Violet's European vacation is history with a murderous twist. Craziness ensues as Violet and Mable continue their adventures. I loved the bus tour characters, and the mysterious things they got up to which lead to the even bigger mystery. A fun read, loved it!"*

-Yvonne Rediger
Author of the Musgrave Landing Mysteries & The Adam Norcross Mysteries

Copyright © 2025 by Joan Havelange
Cover Design by Shelley Havelange
All cover art copyright © 2025
All Rights Reserved
Print ISBN: 978-1-998725-00-7
eBook ISBN: 978-1-998725-01-4
First Publication: September 2021
Second Publication: March 2025

All rights reserved under the International and Pan-American Copyright Conventions. No part of this book may be reproduced or transmitted in any form or by any means, electronic or mechanical, including photocopying, recording, or by any information storage and retrieval system, without permission in writing from the publisher.

All rights reserved. Without limiting the rights under copyright reserved above, no part of this publication may be reproduced, stored in, or introduced into a retrieval system, or transmitted, in any form, or by any means (electronic, mechanical, photocopying, recording, or otherwise) without the prior written permission of both the copyright owner and the publisher of this book.

This is a work of fiction. Names, places, characters, and incidents are either the product of the author's imagination or are used fictitiously, and any resemblance to any actual persons, living or dead, businesses, organizations, events, or locales is entirely coincidental. All trademarks, service marks, registered trademarks, and registered service marks are the property of their respective owners and are used herein for identification purposes only. The publisher does not have any control over or assume any responsibility for author or third-party websites or their contents.

**Published by Brown Wolf Publishing**
**Saskatchewan, Canada**

## *Dedication*

To Rosa and the Usual Suspects.

# Prologue Moscow

Mabel bit her lip as she looked at the white, waxy face of the dead woman lying on the bed. The life force that was Hilda drained away, her eyes wide open, sunk back into her skull, jaw slackened, and lips pale. "Come on, we have to get the hell out of here."

"Shouldn't we look for clues first?" Violet asked.

"Clues, what clues? We just erased them."

"But don't you want to find out who killed Hilda?"

"We're in a foreign country." Mabel started for the door.

"That never stopped you before."

"This time, we are in big trouble."

"Why? We didn't do anything wrong," insisted Violet.

Mabel paused, grim-faced; she looked back at the dead woman. "Really! We haven't done anything wrong? We moved a dead body and interfered in a crime scene."

# Chapter One

Mabel looked out of the round window of the plane. The small jetliner flew over the open water on its final approach to Copenhagen airport. She could see the tall wind generators. Denmark's offshore wind farms. The long flight from Toronto, Canada, to Frankfurt, Germany, was behind her. Mabel's tiredness faded, and her excitement grew. Soon, she and Violet would embark on their Nordic adventure.

Mabel's best friend and travelling companion, Violet Ficher, spread their tour travel map on the small lap table.

"Table trays up," instructed a small blonde flight attendant.

"Oh, sorry." Violet's face reddened as she flipped the table back up, fastening it. The two retired nurses were chalk and cheese. Mabel, who barely reached five feet in height, was portly with short snow-white hair. Violet was a tall, thin, athletic woman with fiery red hair from a bottle. Mabel, a widow, cared little about what people thought of her. While Violet, a three-time divorced woman and a stickler for cleanliness bordering on a phobia, never bent the rules. Unlike Mabel, who thought rules were more of a suggestion. Despite their differences, they were fast friends.

Mabel chuckled. "You probably have the trip memorized."

"Probably." Violet conceded; she closed the pamphlet, sticking it into her backpack. Shoving the bag under the seat in front of her, she recited the tour schedule. "Copenhagen, of course, is our first destination. Then on to Gothenburg, Sweden, Oslo, Norway, and then back to Stockholm, Sweden." She took a package of hand wipes from her pocket and plucked one out, cleaning her hands. "And we have an overnight cruise to Helsinki, Finland. Then Russia, Saint Petersburg and then our final destination, Moscow." Violet offered an alcohol wipe to Mabel.

Mabel quickly wiped her hands and took her phone from her pocket, grinning proudly. "Guess what I have? I have a translator app on my phone," she said.

"I hope your phone is on airplane mode."

"It is. But are you amazed?"

"Frankly, yes. Not that long ago, you were a Luddite. You didn't even own a cell phone."

"Well, no more, I'm now a nerd."

Adjusting her blue-framed glasses on her nose, Violet looked down at Mabel's phone. "I doubt that. You still have that old wall phone in your house, but tell me about this app."

"It's great, and even better, it's free. I type in a phrase in English, and it comes up in the language I want. For instance, I have it set for Danish. And as soon as we land, I'm going to type in something, and ta-da, my phone will speak in Danish."

---

COPENHAGEN'S AIRPORT, a bright modern glass and steel facility, was a busy, noisy place. Mabel descended the stairs with Violet and their fellow passengers toward the crowded luggage carousel. At the bottom of the stairs, tour guides held up signs with their tour names. Front and center of the group stood a large woman with a ruddy complexion. Beside her was a thin, athletic-looking girl with long blonde hair. The girl held up the sign with the name of their tour group.

"Hi, I think we're on your tour," Violet greeted, setting her backpack on the floor beside her.

The big-boned woman with dark brown hair turned to the girl with the sign. "Annika, check to see if these women are on our list."

Annika, a girl in her mid-twenties with big blue eyes and a ready smile, stuck her sign in a bag by her feet. "Hello," she greeted. "Welcome to Copenhagen. My name is Annika Nilsson, and —"

"Just check the names. We can exchange pleasantries later," the stout older woman instructed, looking at her watch.

Annika held up a clipboard, smiling apologetically, and asked, "Your names, please?"

Mabel quickly began to tap on her phone. She held up the phone, and a robotic voice spoke in Danish.

Annika grinned and cleared her throat. "Your phone said you were a marble locked inside a hall."

"Darn, spell check. I must have typed in the wrong phrase. My name is Mabel Havelock," Mabel replied, frowning at her phone.

"And I'm Violet Ficher," Violet added, adjusting the straps of her backpack.

"Thank you," Annika said, placing a checkmark beside their names.

## THE SUSPECTS 9

"Good, come. Now we go get your baggage. You are the last members of the tour to arrive. We must not tarry. The other people in my group are waiting on the motorcoach. Follow me," commanded the intimidating, stocky woman.

Mabel tapped on her phone. Stepping in front of the older woman, she held up her phone and grinned as the phone spoke in the same robotic tone.

Annika giggled. The other woman did not. "You want me to wash your shoes?"

"Oh, sorry, my fingers must be hitting the wrong buttons. I was asking what your name is?"

"Forget your toy. I am well-versed in English. My name is Hilda Karlson, and I am your tour director. Enough chit-chat. Follow me."

"It's not a toy," disputed Mabel; pursing her lips, she stuck her phone in her pocket.

"Maybe don't use your phone; that app might not be the best. After all, it is a freebie," cautioned Violet.

"Nonsense, it's fine. I'll get the hang of it. People appreciate it when you try to speak their language." Mabel grabbed the handle of her carry-on bag.

"You're not speaking Danish. Your phone is, and obviously, not doing it well." Violet shifted her backpack, following the tour guide and Annika.

With long, determined strides, Hilda pushed her way through the groups of travellers to the luggage turnstile. Violet's bag was already circling on the carousel. Violet pulled it off, and they waited for Mabel's luggage to come down the chute. Bag after bag tumbled down, and passengers claimed their suitcases. But Mabel's suitcase did not appear.

The turnstile stopped turning. Hilda tapped her foot, looking at her watch. "Your luggage, it is not here," Hilda said gruffly, shifting the strap of a big black satchel on her shoulder.

"Yes, I can see that. Now what?"

Hilda blew out a long breath. "The now what. Is this will delay us even more. I have a schedule to keep. This is causing me precious time. First, you are late, and now I must take you to your airline's lost luggage counter."

"Sorry we didn't arrive on time, but it's the airlines' fault. And I didn't lose my luggage. The airline did," mumbled Mabel.

"Don't mumble. What did you say?"

"I said I didn't lose my suitcase; the airline did."

"Of course, the airline did. Did I say you had?"

"No." Mabel's face flushed.

"Good. Now, Annika, I want you to take this woman." Hilda gestured to Violet. "Escort her to the motorcoach. And I will take this one to the lost luggage counter."

This one! Mabel's hackles rose, but she clamped her lips shut and followed Hilda. The broad-shouldered woman elbowed her way through the crowd. Pulling her carry-on bag, Mabel raced to keep up. "Please, could you slow down," she requested.

"Do not dawdle. We have a schedule to maintain. If you cannot manage that little bag, give the small bag to me."

Mabel sped up. Be darned if she was going to give this cranky woman her bag. At the counter, Mabel took out her phone and began to text.

"Put that phone away," Hilda said, her lips tightened in a firm line. "I don't have time for your silly toy. I will deal with this."

Mabel, disregarding Hilda's instruction, quickly finished texting on her phone. She held it up, waiting for it to speak to the agents. A picture of a red sports car speeding across a desert appeared on her phone. Speaking in Danish, a deep man's voice was apparently explaining the car's benefits.

Hilda sighed loudly, shook her head, and looked at the attendants behind the counter. "See what I put up with day after day?" speaking in English, she asked.

The attendants smiled politely in return.

"Your airline has lost this woman's luggage." Hilda turned to Mabel. "Now put that phone away and pay attention. And give these people your airline ticket receipts. They need your flight numbers."

Mabel frowned at her phone. Darn the ads. Maybe a free app wasn't the way to go. Jamming the phone into her pocket, she opened her purse, piling Kleenex, lip gloss, hand wipes, and scraps of receipts from fast-food places onto the counter. The uniformed woman and the man behind the lost luggage counter grinned.

Hilda gave Mabel a scathing look. "You have lost your airline ticket receipts. You have made a big disaster. It is going to take me forever to fix this." She took out her phone. "I will call Annika; she must now take my tour group to the hotel. I will have to stay with you and sort out your mess. And then you and I will have to take a taxi. Time squandered, and money spent unnecessarily."

Mabel glared back. It wasn't her fault she lost her luggage. Okay, it's her fault she lost her ticket stubs. But did this woman have to be so nasty? She dumped her purse, shaking it upside down. The airline ticket stubs floated out onto the counter. "Ha," she exclaimed.

Hilda put her phone back in her jacket pocket. "Good. At last, the ticket receipts. Now, you must let these good peoples do their jobs."

"I'm not stopping them," grumbled Mabel, stuffing her belongings back in her purse.

Hilda's thin, prominent nose twitched; she tapped a rapid tattoo with her toe. "Do not mumble."

"Please describe your suitcase," requested the agent behind the counter. His partner, typing on a computer, looked up expectantly.

"It's black and about this big." Mabel spread her hands.

"This big is not a measurement." Hilda glanced at her watch; her lips pursed.

"We have pictures," the agent said. He placed a plasticized card on the desk with pictures of luggage with their dimensions.

"This one looks like it," Mabel said, pointing. "Oh, and my bag has a red maple leaf luggage tag too."

"Very good, we will add that to the information. As soon as your bag arrives, we will forward it to your hotel. If we could please have the name of your hotel."

Hilda rummaged in her shoulder bag and took out sheets of paper separating them. She handed one page to the agent. "This is the list of hotels we will be staying for the duration of the tour and the dates." The tour director didn't wait for the agent's response. Instead, she turned, threading her way through the airport crowds. "Come," she called over her shoulder.

Mabel ran to keep up. This was not a good way to begin the tour. Hilda was the tour director; it didn't bode well if there was acrimony. Determined to make peace, she said, "It was so very helpful of you to give the agents the names of all the hotels on our tour. Just in case my baggage doesn't come today."

Hilda grunted in reply.

Mabel bit her lip. Maybe Hilda was just not good at taking compliments. Either the woman never got many, or the tour guide was irritable because she messed up the schedule.

"This is my job. I am a professional," snorted Hilda. "This is not the first piece of luggage that has gone missing."

The big glass doors opened, and they sped out of the airport to the parking lot. The mid-May sun shone brightly down, heat wafting up from the tarmac. A slight breeze rippled Mabel's hair, and her granny glasses slid down her nose; her little carry-on bumped over the hot pavement as she jogged behind Hilda. The woman set a fast pace, winding her way past a myriad of tour buses to the waiting green and yellow bus with the tour logo displayed on the side. A man and a woman with backpacks lying by their feet were standing outside the bus, talking to a tall, blond man in his mid-thirties, wearing a blue uniform with a small name tag. The uniformed man leaning up against the bus stood as Mabel and Hilda approached. He gave a little salute and climbed on board the bus. The couple turned, glancing at Hilda and Mabel, picking up their backpacks; they followed the man onto the bus.

Mabel tugged on her small black bag up to the steps of the bus.

"No, leave your bag here. Bjorn will put it under the bus with the rest of the luggage," directed Hilda.

Relieved, Mabel climbed aboard the bus to a round of applause from the waiting passengers. She smiled; what a friendly group. She slipped down the aisle to sit beside a sullen Violet, who had a scowl on her face. "Are you mad at me?" Mabel asked.

"No, why do you think I'm mad at you?"

"You didn't clap, and you look kind of sour."

"That applause wasn't a welcome greeting. The blonde girl wearing the baseball cap suggested everyone clap. Not because they were happy to see you, but to draw attention to you because you held up the bus."

Mabel, face flushed with embarrassment, looked around at her fellow passengers and grimaced. She guessed she could understand their frustration, but it wasn't her fault the airline lost her luggage. The blonde-haired girl with the baseball cap tipped it, grinning slyly.

Hilda picked up a handheld mike. Turning it on, she tapped on it. Then, leaning close to Annika, she asked. "Did you introduce Bjorn? And did you tell the people where we are going and what is on the agenda for this evening?"

"No," answered Annika. "I thought you would want to do that."

"That is negligence; you should have done the introduction. What were you doing? Just sitting here waiting for me? I'm disappointed in you. It is a good thing I am a forgiving person." Hilda turned to the tour group and raised her mike. "Welcome to Denmark. You met me when you arrived, but the airport is such a busy and noisy place, so you might not have heard my name properly. As you can see on my name tag, my name is Hilda Karlson. I am your tour director."

She patted her lapel. There was no tag. Hilda's lips turned down. She continued. "And this is Annika Nilsson, my apprentice. And as you can see by her ineptness, it will be a long while before she becomes a tour director."

Annika's face reddened; she stared down at her hands. The tour group exchanged embarrassed glances.

Hilda continued, "Our coach driver is Bjorn Hanson. Bjorn will be our driver for the duration of our tour, all the way to Russia." Hilda paused. Her stern countenance disappeared, her face lit up, and her eyes sparkled as she directed a big, warm smile at the driver. "You may clap for Bjorn. And don't forget, at the end of your tour, to tip this man well. Bjorn has made this trip to Russia many, many times. He is an excellent driver. We are in safe hands."

Everyone clapped enthusiastically.

Bjorn stood up from his seat and turned to face the passengers. The tall, athletic, blond-haired man with a ruddy complexion and sparkling blue eyes smiled, revealing even white teeth. "Velkommen," he said with a slight bow. "Which means welcome in Danish."

"Thank you, Bjorn." Hilda's warm smile disappeared from her face. She turned to the group. "I will check you into the hotel and assign you your sleeping rooms. I am sorry you had to wait so long." The tour director nodded in Mabel's direction. "I had to help this lady. She lost her baggage, which is not the fault of my tour company, but I have fixed everything. We go now to the hotel."

The bus started up.

"Wait, wait." Mabel leaped up from her seat. "Stop, stop, my bag isn't on the bus. It's sitting outside on the pavement."

# Chapter Two

As Bjorn brought the bus to a stop. Hilda sighed. "Please put the woman's carryall on the bus," she instructed the driver. Then, turning to look down the aisle at Mabel, she added, "You are responsible for your hand luggage. There are thirty-five other people on this tour. I cannot hold your hand."

"But you told me to leave it outside," protested Mabel.

"Mrs. Havelock, you must pay attention to what I say. I did not tell you to leave your bag on the tarmac. You have already lost one suitcase. Do you want to lose another?"

Mabel gave Hilda a stony look and pressed her lips shut. She had not misheard.

Violet looked sympathetically at Mabel and squeezed her hand. "Please don't make waves; it's our first day. It will get better."

In short order, Bjorn returned, winking good-naturedly at Mabel; he stowed the bag on the luggage rack above her head. Retaking his position behind the steering wheel, he skillfully maneuvered the bus from amid the other tour buses in the parking lot onto the busy highway.

Sitting in the front seat by the door, Hilda held up a glossy brochure over her head, waving it. "This is the itinerary for our tour. Hand out these information sheets, Annika."

Annika jumped up from her seat behind the driver, and with a fist full of pamphlets in her hand, she swayed down the aisle, giving each tour member a brochure.

"We have a lot to cover on this tour. This is vital information. It is the information for the entire trip. I will post the daily itinerary in the lobby of each hotel we stay at. Everyone must pay attention to the schedule I post. Our tour name and number will be on the top of the daily schedule," instructed Hilda. "It is up to you to remember the name and number of our tour. If you get on the wrong bus, that is your fault."

The passengers on the bus murmured to each other as they read the leaflet.

"Pay attention," Hilda said in a firm, commanding voice. "This is essential information I am giving you. You can read your brochure later."

Everyone quieted down except a handsome man with a hint of stubble on his chin. The man with neatly combed dark hair and white streaks at his temples continued to talk to the woman sitting beside him. Spreading the glossy brochure on his knee, he said, "Look, the statue of The Little Mermaid. It is one of the sites we're going to see in Copenhagen. Do you know why they made this little mermaid statue?"

The woman shook her head.

"It's from the Disney movie," the man said.

Hilda stood up and turned to face the passengers. "Mister?" she looked first at the man, then down at her clipboard.

The man continued to talk to his seat companion, "A nice tip of the hat to Disney, don't you think?"

"You, Mr. Talking Man. What is your name?" Hilda asked in a sharp tone.

The man with piercing blue eyes looked through his steel-rimmed glasses down the aisle at Hilda. "Me?" he asked. "Are you, by chance, talking to me?"

"Why yes, by chance I am. What is your name?" Hilda's ruddy cheeks became redder.

"My name is Herman Chapman, and this is my lovely wife, Carmilla," he said, indicating the plump woman wearing a bright floral dress.

The woman, with short, wispy blonde hair, a flushed face, and small brown eyes, looked adoringly at her handsome husband.

"Herman." Hilda knelt in her seat, looking back at the man. Her voice had a steely edge to it. "May I call you Herman?"

"Yes, you may," Herman said. Using his middle finger, he pushed his glasses up on his nose.

Mabel looked across the aisle at Herman. The man looked like a professor or a businessman. He must be teasing his wife.

"First of all, Herman, that hideous Disney version of The Little Mermaid bears minimal resemblance to the actual story written by Hans Christian Andersen, a Dane. The statue is in honour of Han's story. It's not that tacky tale by Disney. And more importantly. When I am talking, it is not because I am fond of my voice. It is important information. Information that your fellow travellers need to hear, even if you do not. So please be quiet."

Herman's blue eyes narrowed as he folded his arms across his chest. He stuck out his stubbled chin and gave his wife a sidelong look. Carmilla laid her head against his shoulder and patted his hand.

The blonde-haired girl with the baseball cap murmured, "I liked the Disney movie."

Hilda cast a dismissive look at the girl. "We will arrive at our hotel shortly." She sighed and continued, "We are already late, so pay attention. You must wait in the lobby to be assigned to your sleeping rooms. Do not rush up to the front desk for your keys. That is my responsibility. After you freshen up, we will all meet in the lobby." Hilda's long nose twitched as she looked at her watch. "We will meet in the lobby precisely at five-thirty. Then we will all walk to the restaurant for our '*Get to Know You Dinner.*' And as for you stragglers." Hilda cast another cold, disdainful glance in Mabel's direction. "The name of the restaurant is in your brochure. Do not lose your brochure. The dinner is booked for six-thirty, so please do not be late."

The bus drove down the broad streets of Copenhagen. Mabel noted the bicycles seemed to outnumber the cars. The lane for the bikes was wide. It appeared to be wider than the lanes for the automobiles. Tall, three and four-story houses lined the streets. They were similar in shape and size, with red-tiled roofs. The plain and unadorned houses were painted brilliant red, blue, green, and even yellow.

The bus parked at the curb in front of a square, white, five-story hotel. And everyone gathered their belongings. Bjorn, the first one off the bus, opened the big luggage door under the bus, and the porters from the hotel rushed out to take the baggage.

Hilda stood at the front of the bus, blocking the exit door and addressing the tour group, some already standing in the aisle. "You will follow me into the lobby, and remember, do not rush up to the desk and ask for your keys. I will get your keys and sort you out. And do not go and grab your luggage. The porters will deliver the bags to your sleeping room. And for God's sake, do not phone down to the desk as soon as you get to your sleeping room. Your luggage can not beat you to your sleeping room." She looked sternly at the group. "Do you understand?"

The blonde girl with the baseball hat giggled.

"You think this information is funny?" Hilda glared at the girl.

The girl shook her head, "No, it's just you keep saying sleeping rooms."

"What do you do in these rooms? You sleep in them. In the dining room, you dine. I see nothing funny. Now, does everyone remember my instructions?" Hilda waited for the course of meek yeses from the passengers. "Good, now, follow me."

Annika sped across the lobby to the desk as Mabel, Violet, and their fellow tour members trooped into the hotel, standing obediently away from the front desk. Hilda stationed herself at a glass and silver coffee table, waiting. The pretty blonde girl hurried back with sheets of paper and keycards, placing them on the table in front of Hilda.

"Is there a chance to do some shopping before dinner?" A big-bosomed woman asked.

Hilda shuffled the papers in front of her. "Dinner or shopping, you pick."

"Ah, dinner, I guess."

"I'm so pleased to hear that," Hilda said sarcastically, her lips curled down. "Now, if you have read the brochure, you will know this is an overnight stop. Tomorrow we will visit the Copenhagen sights. And tomorrow evening, when we return, your supper will be on your own. This hotel has a wonderful dining room, so if you don't want to venture out, you will enjoy dining here."

"Will we have to pay for our dinner?" asked Herman.

"Yes, you must pay for your dinner. But not this evening. This evening, the meal is included in the tour package." Hilda held up a hand, her palm facing the tour group. "And before I give you your keys, there is one more detail you must pay attention to. Not tomorrow morning. But the following morning, you must have your suitcases outside your sleeping room before breakfast. The porters will collect your luggage and put them on the bus. Is that clear?"

"Tomorrow morning," Carmilla said.

"No, I distinctly said not tomorrow morning. The following morning, we are leaving for Oslo, the capital of Norway."

"What day is that?" asked the blonde girl with the baseball cap.

"I cannot hold your hand. Read the poster on the bulletin board. It explains the schedule. Do you all understand?" She looked at the tour group standing before her. The members nodded meekly. "Good, that's settled." Hilda nodded back and looked down at the list of names on the papers in her hand. "Now, please listen carefully. I will call your name and give you your keys." The tour group surged forward, crowding around the coffee table. "Stay back and listen for your names. I have a loud voice. For God's sake, be calm," she reprimanded. "You will all get your key."

Mumbling and grumbling, the tour members stepped back from the table. "Mabel Hitchcock and Violet Ficher," Hilda called out.

"My name is Havelock," protested Mabel, threading her way through the crowd to claim the room key.

"I read out your name. Now take your key," snapped Hilda. "People are waiting."

Mabel peered down at the sheet of paper, trying to read how her name was spelled on the list. But quickly stood back as Hilda, with a warning look in her eyes, held out the keycard.

Violet squeezed Mabel's shoulder. "Never mind. Let's go to our room."

"That woman is impossible," Mabel fumed, following Violet across the crowded lobby to a bank of four elevators. Two men in suits pulling big black suitcases shouldered their way past the women and dumped their large bags in front of them.

Mabel sighed, more rudeness. This will be a tour to remember for all the wrong reasons, she thought, as she listened to the men conversing in Danish. An elevator door opened, and the men stepped politely back, allowing Mabel and Violet to precede them into the elevator. Violet nodded her thanks and used her knuckle to press the number for their floor. The elevator stopped at the third floor, and they stepped around the men's large bags out into the hallway.

"This direction, I think the room numbers get bigger this way," Violet said, leading the way down the hallway. She stopped at their room, inserted the keycard through the card reader, and opened the door. "I like this room. It's nice, modern, and clean," she remarked, setting her backpack on a bed.

The room's white, grey and silver decor was bright and airy. Mabel opened her small carry-on, dumping the contents on a bed and taking stock of her belongings. She took out a sweater, a nightgown, a pair of socks, her toiletry bag, two paperback mystery novels, three rolls of toilet tissue, a box of Kleenex, and an extra pair of walking shoes.

"You definitely have the paper products covered. Why so many? We aren't doing a tour of a third-world country. We're in Europe."

"If I'd known the airline was going to lose my baggage, I would have packed less toilet paper and more clothes," Mabel muttered.

Violet opened her backpack and took out a container of alcohol wipes.

"I suppose you have a change of clothes in your backpack."

"Well, yes, I have. And as you have just found out, you can't be too careful." Violet opened the yellow cylinder, drawing out a wad of wipes.

"Lesson learned," Mabel sighed. "Too bad we aren't the same size."

"Never mind, I'm sure your suitcase will turn up shortly," Violet said as she proceeded to wipe the doorknobs and light switches.

"I'm not a big fan of Hilda, our tour guide," Mabel grumbled, putting the rolls of toilet tissue back in her carry-on.

"Give Hilda time. She is under pressure and is trying to get us organized."

"I guess so. She did sort out my lost luggage. But charm sure isn't her long suit."

"Hilda has a lot on her plate. I think getting all of us from point A to point B is kind of like herding cats," Violet said, taking out more alcohol wipes from the cylinder.

Mabel chuckled. "You did say this was a nice, clean hotel room."

"One can never be too careful." Violet continued around the room, wiping surfaces.

# Chapter Three

Mabel showered and donned her jeans and her white and navy stripe T-shirt. She brushed her short, white hair and sighed. "It's hard to feel clean when you're wearing the same clothes you've been in for a day and a night," she said, laying Violet's hairbrush on the glass-topped dressing table.

Violet, wearing a pair of grey slacks and a long-sleeved yellow blouse, took a silky blue scarf from her suitcase. "Here, drape this around your neck. It may not make you feel like you are wearing clean clothes, but it will give you the appearance that you are."

Mabel accepted the scarf, wrapping it loosely around her neck. "You think so?"

"I know so. You look fine. And who knows, maybe your luggage has arrived. We should stop by the desk and ask on our way out to supper," Violet said, her hand on the doorknob.

Mabel followed Violet down the corridor. "I hope the rest of the crew aren't all dressed to the nines."

A family of four waiting for the elevator smiled a greeting. The children were chatting excitedly with their parents in Danish. The elevator doors opened, and everyone crowded in. "Come in; there is room for all," encouraged the tall woman with a Danish accent, ushering her son and small daughter toward the back of the elevator. As Violet and Mabel joined them, Mabel recognized four Australians from their tour group as they squeezed in beside them. The little girl wrinkled her forehead, gazing curiously up at Violet, who pressed the lobby button with a pen in her hand. Violet smiled down at the child and slipped the pen into her purse. "The pen is a precaution against germs," she said. The child grinned.

"You are tourists. How do you like Copenhagen?" the towering Danish man asked.

"We've just arrived. How did you know we are tourists?" asked Mabel.

"Oh, it's not hard." Chuckled the man as the elevator door opened.

"I wonder how he knew. Do we look like tourists?" Mabel asked Violet as the family crossed the lobby to the front door.

"I reckon because you are speaking English, or maybe the pen gave you away," drawled the lanky Australian man, laughing as he followed his companions to join the tour members waiting in the lounge.

"He's probably right, anyway. Let's see if your suitcase has arrived."

Mabel approached the front desk. "My name is Mabel Havelock. Have any suitcases been delivered here with my name tag on the bag?" Mabel spelt out her name.

A courteous little man conferred with his two colleagues and then turned back to Mabel. "I am sorry, no luggage has been delivered," he apologized.

"If my suitcase comes while we are out for supper, would you have it sent to our room?"

"Supper?"

"Dinner," supplied Violet.

"Yes, of course, madam," the man replied.

Mabel thanked him, and they crossed the lobby to join the tour group. Not everyone had changed clothes. The couple, wearing sporty khaki vests with many zippers, stood talking with Bjorn, the bus driver, wearing a bright red sports jacket with the tour company's logo on the breast pocket. He seemed intent on what the couple was saying. Nearby, a group of women dressed in brilliant saris and men in casual slacks and dress shirts. A group of young Japanese men and women sported trendy pants and shirts. Mabel wondered if some of the young people had colds. Three of them wore blue cotton facemasks. She briefly mused what it would look like if everyone wore a face mask. She dismissed the thought. What a silly idea. Instead, she marvelled at the mixture of the languages spoken. Everyone was in good spirits, laughing and intermingling: a thirty-five-member tour group, a mini-united nation.

Hilda, attired in a blazer in the same shade of red as the bus driver, alit from an elevator and strode across the lobby. Annika, also dressed in a red linen jacket, followed in her wake. The only difference was that Hilda wore blue slacks, and Annika wore a blue skirt in the same shade of blue. Bjorn strolled over to join them.

"Come, people, you must follow me," directed Hilda. "It is a short walk. Here in Denmark, we like to walk or ride our bikes."

"You will notice it is incredibly quiet on our streets. Because, of course, we have almost more bikes than cars. And you will not see so many car parks. Instead, there are many bike parks." Annika added.

"I find that hard to believe," snorted Herman; taking his wife by the arm, he propelled her forward. Carmilla's short legs struggled to keep up.

"It is true. People have at least two bikes. Bikes that they ride to work and bikes for pleasure. We are a healthy nation," Annika said proudly.

And it was quiet, but Mabel was used to quietness. She lived in a little farming community on the Canadian prairies. She and the rest of the group hurried to keep up with the tour director's long strides.

An exuberant, tall, skinny head waiter at the restaurant greeted Hilda. "Our famous smorgasbord awaits you," he proclaimed.

Mabel grinned and nudged Violet. "This maître d' could double for Ichabod Crane."

"Shush," scolded Violet.

"Please, please, come this way." The gangly man hurried them through the long dining room with multiple tables to a smaller area. Where round tables covered in white linen tablecloths were set in a semi-circle. The tables flanked long buffet tables laden with hot meats and vegetables in stainless steel chafing dishes, large soup tureens, and a long salad bar. "You see, all is ready for you, my dear Hilda."

Hilda gave the man a big smile and motioned for the tour group to find a table.

Mabel and Violet sat at a table close to the windows with four couples and one lone man. While waiting for the go-ahead to partake of the smorgasbord, each person introduced themselves. The first was the talkative man.

Mabel, already familiar with Herman, the know-it-all, listened as he introduced himself. "My name is Professor Chapman, but you may call me Herman or Professor." He chuckled and continued. "And this is my little woman, Carmilla."

Carmilla beamed adoringly at her husband.

Across the table sat the couple with the khaki vests. Their attire looked perfect for travelling. Mabel wished she'd packed vests, but now she would settle for just getting her suitcase. The man wearing the vest with a closely cropped brush-cut said, "My name is Allan Hughes, and this is my wife, Bridget." Allan, the slender man with a smooth, tanned face, grinned and added. "My wife Bridget and I like to think of ourselves as gypsies travelling the world."

Bridget, the athletic-looking woman, had blue-framed glasses like Violet. Her long ginger hair framed her thin, angular face. She removed her glasses, wiped the lenses with her white linen napkin, and smiled. "That's us, two nomads travelling the world."

Sitting beside them was a slight-built man with sparse reddish-brown hair. His ears stuck out in a sugar-bowl fashion. He cleared his throat. "My name is Fred Schmidt, and this is my wife, Sheila. We are from New Zealand.

Mabel remembered Sheila; she was the big, busty woman who asked if she could shop. The woman had long, straight, mousy brown hair; her bangs brushed the top of her eyebrows, giving her a peculiar look as though peeking through a bush.

Mabel also recognized the girl sitting across the table from her. She was the girl with the baseball hat who organized her welcome aboard the bus. Let bygones be bygones, she told herself.

The squat man next to the girl put his arm around her shoulders. "My name is Sam Morgan, and this is my beautiful Verity," the man said in a deep, raspy voice.

Verity, a svelte girl with long legs wearing a low-cut burgundy dress and long, dangling gold earrings, flashed a bright smile. She tucked a curl of her platinum blonde hair behind her ear. Her bright blue eyes sparkled as she looked at Sam. Mabel suspected Sam was much older than the pretty blond girl. The bald man with a fringe of salt and pepper hair looked like an overweight wrestler. His big head and flat nose reminded Mabel of a British bulldog.

The lone man at the table introduced himself as Leon Peeters. The sandy-haired, short man with faded blue eyes and chubby cheeks barely looked at anyone as he talked.

Mabel took a second look at the little man. Was he wearing a wig? It looked a lot like a wig her uncle Ben used to wear. She glanced at Violet. Did she notice? Leon appeared to be a shy little man with a quiet voice and manner. But they had experience with lone male travellers on their trip to Egypt, and not all were what they seemed to be. And even though the man spoke perfect English. Mabel detected a slight accent, but from what country?

As Violet introduced herself, Mabel's stomach grumbled; she looked around the dining room at the other tables. No one was helping themselves to the buffet. Were they waiting for some sort of signal to start dishing up? Annika, Hilda, and

Bjorn sat at a small table near the back of the room. A waiter was pouring them wine.

"Mabel, say a few words." Violet poked her under the table.

"My name is Mabel Havelock, and I'm from Canada. And this is my first trip to Europe—"

A sharp clinking of metal on glass interrupted Mabel's speech.

"Welcome to Copenhagen," Hilda said, tapping her wineglass with a spoon. Then, with a wineglass in her hand, she continued. "This is the beginning of your Nordic Tour, culminating in Moscow." She raised her glass. The tour group clapped enthusiastically. Hilda beamed at the group seated around the room. "We have a lot to see. So please remember, you must always read the itinerary, and you must always be on time." She took another drink from her glass of wine. Putting her empty wineglass down on the table, she indicated the smorgasbord. "This meal is included in your tour. But if you order drinks of any kind, including soft drinks, you must pay the waiter." With a satisfied smile on her face, the tour director sat. Reaching for the wine bottle on the table, she poured more red wine into her glass. As Hilda settled back in her chair, the rush began to the food table. "Oh, wait, wait." Hilda stood. "I have had Annika write your names on name tags. I suggest you wear them, so you and your fellow travellers get to know each other. Annika, please distribute the name tags now."

Everyone resumed their seats as Annika sped around the room, handing out the name tags.

Hilda banged her knife against her water glass. "You may now eat, and please enjoy your dinner."

The two tables with the Spanish people were first in line, followed by the East Indians. And wedged in between the groups of Asians and the Australians were the people from Mabel's table. Then, bringing up the rear, another group of Americans. Mabel heaped a pile of meatballs in a cream sauce on her plate, adding mashed potatoes and lingonberries. Violet selected the veal in dill sauce and fresh vegetables. Back at the table, everyone ordered cocktails or wine.

Except for Herman, who complained, "We shouldn't have to pay for anything. It said in the pamphlet that dinner and drinks were included. I bet she's splitting the money with the waiters."

Allan, the khaki-wearing man, reached into one of the many pockets in his vest and produced the glossy brochure. "Nope," he said. "It says right here. The Copenhagen get acquainted meal is included in our tour package. But we are responsible for our drinks." He folded the paper and stuck it back in his pocket.

"I guess I should have read the fine print," Herman grumbled.

Allan smirked. "It's written quite clearly."

Giving Allan a sour look, Carmilla squeezed her husband's hand.

The rest of the meal continued affably, each exchanging information. "I'm a retired dentist," Fred, the New Zealander, told them.

"And I was his receptionist; that's how we met. It was love at first sight," Sheila added, helping herself to a chicken leg from Fred's plate.

"I'm a professor of Scandinavian history, now retired," Herman reiterated. "I'm anxious to see the countries I studied and taught firsthand. My dear wife is a stay-at-home mom."

"Our children are now all grown up," Carmilla added shyly.

Leon timidly told them he was a retired insurance salesman. Verity revealed she was a model before she married Sam, and they had no children. Sam said he was a businessman but gave no details. Nor did Allan Hughes. When asked, he reiterated he and his wife were world travellers. Bridget nodded, her green eyes sparkling as she smiled at her travelling companions.

Violet and Mabel related that they were both retired nurses and had been best friends since college, and they lived in a small town in the middle of the Canadian prairies.

After the meal, Mabel excused herself and crossed the room to the table where Annika, Hilda, and Bjorn sat. She approached Hilda and said, "I still don't have my luggage."

Hilda swallowed a gulp of a greenish-coloured cocktail, licked her lips, and then placed her cocktail glass on the table. A sprig of mint fell onto the white linen cloth. "What is it you think I can do? I'm not able to produce your luggage like magic," she said, slurring her words.

"I know it's not your fault. But do you think my bag will be here before we leave Copenhagen? Or should I shop for clothes?"

"My dear womans, how can I possibly know that? I can not hold your hand. If your suitcase does not come and you are happy to wear soiled clothes, come along with us on our tour of Copenhagen. If you want clothes that are not soiled, you must do the shops. You must shop." Hilda tripped over her words. "The concierge at this hotel. At our hotel can, may recommend nice shops." The tour guide licked her lips and exhaled. "But the tour begins tomorrow. We go, we go to see." Hilda frowned, paused, picked up her cocktail glass and then turned to Annika. "Tell her, this womans where we go."

Annika shot Hilda a disapproving look, plucked a sheet of paper from her handbag, and recited the itinerary. "Tomorrow morning, we stop for pictures at The Little Mermaid. Then, we tour the Christiansborg Palace. Our final stop will be at the Kronborg Castle, a UNESCO World Heritage Site. I do hope you come."

"But we will go on the tour with you or without you. It is your choice." Hilda saluted Mabel with her cocktail glass and took a deep drink.

"Yes, thank you. I guess it is." Mabel didn't feel thankful. But if she were to get along with the cranky tour director. She would have to suck it up and play nice. She followed Violet out of the restaurant and down the sidewalk. Night had fallen, but the streets were well-lit and surprisingly noisy. Parties were in full swing at the open-air cafes. "I wish I never asked Hilda about my bag. She has had a tad too much to drink, but she's right; there is no way she would know when the darn thing will show up. I think I'll have to miss tomorrow's tour."

# Chapter Four

Mabel excused herself from the breakfast table and trooped to the hotel's front desk. She took out her phone. Mabel knew the concierge spoke English, but she wanted to see if she could get the hang of her translator app, so she typed, *'My name is Mabel Havelock. Do you have my suitcase?'* She held up her phone; the robotic voice spoke in Danish.

A man picking up a keycard looked at Mabel and grinned.

The receptionist behind the desk made an 'oh' sound. "Madam, I'm not sure I understand. What is it you require? Do you really want a male escort?" she asked in perfect English.

"Good lord, no. No, I don't," sputtered Mabel. "I want my suitcase. The airline was supposed to send my bag here. Has it arrived?"

The woman behind the desk looked relieved. "I'm afraid the app on your phone has made a different request." She giggled. "I'll check on your luggage."

Mabel tapped on her phone while the friendly woman conferred with her colleague. "Stupid app," Mabel muttered.

"I am sorry, no luggage has been delivered for you."

"Okay, thanks anyway." Mabel turned away from the desk as Violet approached with her camera slung over her shoulder.

"I'm going to have to go shopping. I can't stand wearing these clothes another day longer."

"You're going to miss out on the first tour of our trip. Please come."

"Really. If it was you, would you wear clothes you have been wearing for two days?"

Violet didn't hesitate a moment. "Right. I'll take pictures."

Mabel stood on the sidewalk and waved Violet off. Then, she returned to the front desk, took out her phone, and typed, 'Could *you please tell me where I will find clothing stores?*' She paused, pushed delete, and put the phone back in her pocket. After all, the woman did speak English. "Are there clothing stores near this hotel?" she asked.

The woman grinned and wrote out the name of a shop. "It is not far, just a few blocks from here," she said.

The morning rush hour in Copenhagen was in full swing. Bikes and cars streamed down the busy city streets. Mabel waited for a pedestrian light, then crossed and strolled down the sidewalk past the tall, narrow storefronts with small name signs. She stopped at a shop with a big glass window, where mannequins dressed in smart sports clothes posed. It was the shop recommended by the concierge. But moments later, she left without buying anything; the clothes in the shop were all high-end, and she was looking for simple everyday wear.

Mabel wandered the streets, stopping at small shops and large, getting more and more frustrated. When, at last, she found a department store and a clerk who spoke excellent English, she bought an assortment of socks and underpants, three T-shirts and a pair of jeans. Pleased, Mabel returned with her purchases to the hotel and laid her new T-shirts on the bed. A bit of an extravagance, she thought. Her suitcase was probably on the way to the hotel. But the T-shirts were so colourful. At least she only bought one new pair of jeans. Mabel showered, changed into her new red and yellow striped T-shirt, and tugged on her jeans. The jeans were a bit snug, but they would be fine for a day. Sitting on her bed, she looked at her watch. It had only taken her three hours to shop. What was she going to do with the rest of her day? She scanned the tour schedule for Copenhagen. Where would the tour group be? She had no idea, but she was not going to spend the day in her hotel room.

She stopped again at the front desk and asked. "What attraction or tourist sight is nearby?"

The friendly concierge, who'd suggested the clothing shops, placed a small street map on the counter. She picked up a pen and underlined the hotel. "You are here," she said. "And in just a few blocks is our famous Tivoli Gardens." She circled the gardens with the pen.

Mabel happily accepted the map, thanked the woman, and set off. Three blocks from the hotel, she found the Tivoli Gardens, which had a large ornate Moorish arch at the entrance. To her surprise, the garden was an amusement park. She wandered around, taking in the sights. There was an assortment of rides and roundabouts and a variety of roller coasters. The park also had an area with lush flower gardens. Another section with hanging Japanese lanterns. And still, another where she saw Chinese pagodas and lily ponds. The garden was a busy, crowded place with parents and children enjoying the park.

Mabel, delighted with her find, strolled along, looking at the attractions. At a puppet show, she noticed a man wearing an old-fashioned black hat with a brim. What did they call that hat? Was it a trilby? The man appeared to be watching the people instead of the puppet show; she frowned. The skulking man looked a little like Leon.

An iridescent blue peacock strutted in front of her, spreading its feathered tail and displaying blue, gold, and green shimmering eye markings. Mabel reached into her pocket for her phone. Tapping the camera button on her phone, she pointed at the large bird. The peacock stared at her, stretching out its long neck, its sharp black eyes unblinking. The bird, spreading his tail feathers, pranced ominously toward Mabel, emitting shrill shrieks. Mabel backed up. The peacock, tail feather spread out quivering, came closer and closer, screeching piercing: *'eeeiu, eeeiu'* sounds, its beady black eyes fixed menacingly on Mabel. Turning tail, she ran, darting around people who were watching the puppet show. Casting a frightened look over her shoulder, Mabel scurried through the crowd. She spotted an open-air café. Out of breath, she looked around worriedly. There was no sign of the big scary peacock. Relieved, Mabel entered and sat at a table. Instantly, a waiter appeared. She took out her phone, tapped on her translator app, paused, looked at her app, and then back at the waiter. "A coffee, a burger, and fries, please," she asked tentatively.

"Yes, ma'am," the waiter replied in perfect English.

Mabel drank her coffee as she waited for her food, watching the endless stream of people coming and going to the exhibits and rides. Over by the carousel, she spotted Allan and Bridget. Perhaps the tour was stopping here for lunch.

She hollered out, "Hello, you two." But the music from the merry-go-round drowned out her voice. The waiter, with her order, stepped up to her table. As he laid out her cutlery and napkin, she watched the two-some stop to chat and shake hands with a tall man in a long grey coat with a bright red and yellow striped scarf wrapped around his neck. The man appeared to hand a small package to Allan. Mabel chomped down on her burger, looking for more members of her tour group, but she saw none. When she looked back at the carousel, Allan and Bridget were gone.

# Chapter Five

It was early morning, and the sun shone brightly as the passengers climbed aboard the bus, stowing their carry-on in the overhead luggage racks. "Good morning, good morning," greeted Hilda cheerfully. "We have a long journey ahead of us, and I'm as anxious as you to begin our journey." She waited until everyone was seated, smiled, and added. "Please remember where you are seated today, as we have seat rotation. Each day, we rotate the seating. So tomorrow, you will sit two seats back from where you are seated today. For example, if you are sitting up front behind me, you will move to your left and sit two seats back tomorrow. Does everyone understand? Is everyone happy?" Smiling again, she picked up her clipboard.

"What about yesterday? Doesn't that count?" questioned Herman. "I know for a fact that Fred and Sheila were sitting in the front seat behind Annika. It isn't fair. They are sitting there again today."

Hilda's sunny smile evaporated. "Where were you sitting?"

"Right behind you," replied Herman.

Hilda gave Herman a scathing look. "Fine, fine, we will sort this out. But now, thanks to you, we are going to be delayed." She forced a smile. "But of course, we must be fair. Peoples,

# THE SUSPECTS

peoples pay attention. Please go to where you were sitting yesterday."

Sheila nudged Fred, and they exchanged a happy grin.

"What? Why?" asked a tall, gangly Australian man whose name tag read Bert Miller.

"Just do what I ask." Hilda gripped the back of a seat. Her knuckles whitened as she watched the passengers bump into each other, arguing who was sitting where.

"It's people, not peoples," corrected a thin woman whose name tag read Cindy Miller.

"What did you say?" Hilda frowned, her lips forming a thin, tight line.

"Your pronunciation is wrong. You should say people, not peoples."

Hilda glowered at the woman. "Do you speak Danish?"

"Well, no."

Hilda gave Cindy a cold, hard look. "Do you speak any other language? Besides your Australian version of English."

Bjorn tapped a rapid tattoo with his fingers on the steering wheel, then cast a look over his shoulder at Annika. Her head bent, her cheeks flushed, shuffling papers on her lap; she glanced up at Hilda, then quickly back down at her lap.

"What do you mean, my version of English?" Cindy's face reddened.

"No drama, Sheila, get your kit. We're moving seats," drawled Bert.

"Sheila? Your name tag says Cindy. Annika, you mixed up name tags."

Annika's head jerked up. "No, I don't think so?"

"You don't think so!" stormed Hilda.

"Annika didn't mix anything up. Sheila is an expression in our version of English," snapped Cindy.

"Sheila means girl," Bert explained, standing; he grabbed his bag from the overhead rack.

Hilda exhaled a long breath and returned to the front of the bus. The passengers, gathering their belongings, crowded and bumped into each other in the aisle, arguing over who was sitting where.

"Darn Herman. Our tour guide appears to have a short fuse. One minute, she is sunny. The next, she's like a thundercloud," Mabel muttered, following Violet's lead as she had no idea where her friend had sat on the bus. Finally, everyone settled into their seats.

Hilda's lips twisted into a sneer as she looked over the rows of seats at Cindy. "People," she said.

The passengers, rearranging their carry-on, ignored her.

"Stop. Do not store your bag or camera. As I said at the outset, everyone, every day, will move back two seats. Now that you are where you sat yesterday, you must now move two seats; the rotation is to move two seats back."

"What?" grumbled an Asian man wearing a Hawaiian shirt. "You can't be serious."

Hilda looked at his name tag. "Mr. Patel. I'm afraid I am perfectly serious. You must do this. We have had a complaint."

Sheila, the busty Newland woman, grasped her tote bag. Her lips turned down; she glared at Herman. Fred stood, shrugged, and reached overhead for their hand luggage. A bag came down, smacking him on the knee. "Dammit," he swore. His ears turned bright red as he rubbed his knee, casting a disgusted look at Herman. "Idiot," he muttered.

Annika jumped up from her seat. "Everyone, please cooperate. Bjorn is anxious to get us on our trip so you can enjoy the scenic countryside of Denmark," she urged.

The passengers picked up their belongings, muttering and grumbling, giving Herman dirty looks.

Herman, ignoring their stares, protested, "This still can't be right. Carmilla and I should be sitting up front."

Hilda stomped over to loom over Herman. "You will sit here. I will not hear any more petty complaints. My schedule is already off because of you. There will be no more moving. And people, remember where you are sitting. I will not have this again. Does everyone understand?" Hilda stood, arms crossed over her chest, watching the passengers. When they meekly nodded their assent, she strode back to her seat, muttering, "They don't pay me enough for this job."

Angrily, Herman slumped in his seat. Carmilla, lying her head on his shoulder, patted his arm.

Annika stood and turned to face the passengers as the bus pulled out from the curb. With her hand on the back of her seat, she announced, "Dear friends, we are a little behind schedule, but this will be a delightful leg of our trip. You will enjoy our drive through the picturesque countryside of Denmark." The disgruntled passengers settled down as Annika continued, "We have a short ferry ride to Helsingborg, Sweden. In Sweden, we will visit Gothenburg. Then, we go over the border to Oslo, Norway. It is a big day. And we will have two days in Oslo before going to Stockholm."

The passengers rewarded Annika with a smattering of applause.

"We are travelling to Norway, then back to Sweden? Are you sure? That doesn't make sense." Herman's voice trailed off as Hilda stood.

"Are you now a tourism expert?" she asked through closed teeth.

"No, sorry," mumbled Herman.

Hilda's nose flared, her lips twisted into a smirk; she nodded and sat back in her seat.

"Not an auspicious start to the tour, passengers snarling at each other and our tour guide in a snit," Mabel whispered to Violet. She tugged at her jeans; they were clinging to her like a second skin.

Violet shrugged. "I know. They aren't a happy bunch right now, but they'll get over it. It's a tempest in a teapot, as the saying goes. Regardless, you and I shall enjoy this trip."

The bus travelled through the Danish countryside, past green rolling hills, cultivated fields, and farms; some of the small white farmhouses had sod roofs. Mabel grinned. Some roofs needed mowing.

Verity leaned across the aisle and tapped Mabel's arm. "I had my picture taken with the Little Mermaid." She passed her phone to Mabel. "See."

"Good picture," Mabel complemented, returning the phone.

"It's a shame you missed Christiansborg Palace; it was amazing," Verity said, putting her phone in her purse. "But the best was Hamlet's Castle. It was wonderful, wasn't it, Sam?"

Sam, sitting by the window, his head slumped back on the seat, his mouth hanging open, snoring.

"It was a great feeling to walk the battlements that Hamlet walked. A step back in time," Herman agreed.

"That wasn't Hamlet's Castle," Allan voiced from the seat behind Verity. "Kronborg Castle is the Hamlet castle."

"What? No, I'm sure the tour guide told us it was Hamlet's Castle." Verity frowned at Herman.

Herman nodded.

"The Kronborg Castle was the setting for Hamlet. You do know who Shakespeare is?" Allan asked, a sneer in his voice.

Herman glowered. "Of course, I know who William Shakespeare is. And I know Hamlet is fictional. It's a play written by Shakespeare. I never said it was Hamlet's castle; I meant it was the setting for Hamlet."

"Anyway, Allan, didn't you think the castle was the best ever?" Verity asked exuberantly.

"Yes, fascinating," Allan replied in a bored tone. He opened a paperback, taking out a bookmark.

Mabel was sure she'd seen Allan and Bridget at Tivoli Gardens amusement park. But if they were at the castle, she was mistaken. And what about Leon? Maybe she hadn't seen him either.

The bus drove through small villages and past pastoral countryside. Soon, Mabel and most of the bus passengers were fast asleep, only waking when the bus came to a stop. As Bjorn slowly drove the bus onto the ferryboat, Fred stood in the aisle, pulling down a bag, opening it, and taking out another tote bag, handing it to his wife.

"Please wait until the bus comes to a complete stop," instructed Hilda. "Then you may take the stairs to the top deck. When we reach Helsingborg, we will all meet by the bar and proceed back to our bus. Yes?"

Ignoring Hilda's instructions, the passengers stood in the aisle, waiting for the bus door to open. Hilda sighed.

"This is a short ferry ride, but it will give you a chance to stretch your legs," Annika said as they climbed the iron stairs to the deck above. Hilda waved cheerily to the tour members at the top of the stairs and entered a small, overcrowded bar.

"Do they have a gift shop aboard this ferry?" asked Sheila.

"You may find some trinkets. But please remember, you will see a lot of souvenir shops on our tour. This one is small, and it may be a little pricy," replied Annika.

"Come on, Fred, it won't hurt to look." Sheila sped down the deck toward the small, jam-packed souvenir store.

"Yes, dear," Fred said, following his wife.

Everyone dispersed. Allan and Bridget strolled down the deck toward the prow of the boat. Verity lounged on a deck chair beside Herman and a young Japanese couple. Mrs. Patel followed Sheila and Fred to the gift shop. Verity's husband, Sam, stood in the canteen line behind Carmilla.

Mabel and Violet wandered along the deck; they passed Annika, leaning against the deck railing, laughing at something Leon was saying. Mabel was tempted to ask him how he liked the Tivoli Gardens. But then she had thought she'd seen Allan and Bridget, and they had been on the tour to the Christiansborg Palace and Kronborg Castle. So it was best not to say anything. But what if he had been the man she saw? As she walked alongside Violet, Mabel debated whether she should tell Violet about the mystery man.

"I'm loving this trip. I'm sorry you missed the tour yesterday. It couldn't have been much fun for you," Violet said.

Mabel paused, resting her arms on the railing, watching Denmark fade into the horizon. Looking skyward at the big white fluffy clouds, listening to a flock of seagulls' cries as they circled, following fishing boats out to sea. "No, but I made the best of it. The Tivoli Gardens were kind of neat."

Violet ran a hand along the deck rail, brushing off her hands, and said, "This is the way to travel."

"I agree," Mabel said, tilting her head back, feeling the sun's warmth on her face, enjoying the sea breeze.

"And I'm so pleased nothing has awoken that suspicious nature of yours. Not like our trip to Egypt. Promise you won't start detecting."

"Oh, no detecting, I promise. I'm just taking in the sights. But by the way, did Allan and Bridget take the tour with you yesterday?"

"Yes, they were on the bus when we left the hotel. Why do you ask?"

"And they were there for the entire tour?"

"I guess so. Probably, but after the palace tour, I couldn't say. I never really paid attention. I was more interested in the sights than who was with us."

"And Leon, did you see him?"

"Why? Why are you asking about these people?"

"I thought I saw them all at the amusement park."

"Geez, Mabel, you said you would just enjoy the sights. Are you looking for trouble?"

"I'm not looking for trouble."

"The sights, just the sights, remember?"

"Yes, yes, the sights. I'm just curious, and I'm most likely mistaken," replied Mabel. But maybe she wasn't, and if she wasn't, what did that mean? Or did it mean anything? She pushed the thoughts from her mind; it wasn't any of her business. She'd promised Violet.

# Chapter Six

Annika picked up the microphone, tapped on it, and began. "Welcome to Oslo, the capital of Norway." Waking everyone up, including Hilda, who had fallen asleep the moment they boarded the bus. As the bus travelled over a busy bridge, Annika continued in a bright, cheery voice. "You will see many marvellous bridges in this charming city. If you look out your windows, you will glimpse the enchanting islands that surround Oslo. The islands are all easily accessible; island hopping is a popular tourist activity. And day trips are available. But unfortunately, not for us; we have a very busy schedule."

Mabel wriggled in her seat, sucking in her gut and surreptitiously buttoning her jeans. She couldn't wait to get off the bus. They'd travelled all day. The stop in Gothenburg, Sweden, had only been a lunch break.

She treaded behind Violet as they followed their fellow passengers into the hotel lobby. Mabel ignored Hilda's instructions to stay in the lounge and skirted around Sheila. Sheila was lugging a cloth bag filled with the souvenirs she'd picked up on the ferry. Mabel followed Annika to the check-in desk, waited until she left with the list of rooms and keycards, and then inquired about her luggage. The people behind the desk conferred before telling her no, luggage wasn't waiting for her. Disgruntled, she followed Annika back to the lounge, where Hilda, sitting behind a small wooden desk, took a sip from a silver flask. The woman was laughing and chatting with the tour passengers.

"Thank you, Annika, you are always so efficient," Hilda said, accepting the list of rooms and keys.

Annika beamed happily.

"There is a special dinner tonight," Hilda announced, smiling at the tour group gathered around her. "You will love the setting and the meal. And you will be pleased to know the meal is covered in your tour package."

"What about drinks? Are drinks included?" asked Herman.

Hilda's smile turned into a grimace. "Read your brochure," she snapped. She then turned to the rest of the tour members, inhaled, paused, and a faint smile reappeared on her lips. "Please do not be tardy; we have tables reserved. Tomorrow, we have a busy day. We will go to Frogner Park, the Royal Palace, and the Viking Museum. Now, I call your name. Allan and Bridget Hughes."

Allan sprinted up, accepting the room keycard.

Hilda's eyes narrowed as she selected another keycard and looked over at Mabel. "Where were you? You went to the desk. I distinctly told everyone to wait with me in the lobby while Annika deals with the reservations."

Mabel's hackles rose. She wasn't a child. "If you know where I went, why do you ask? But if you want to know why, I'll tell you. I was asking if my suitcase had caught up with us. And, of course, it hasn't."

## THE SUSPECTS

"You are blaming me?"

"I never said that. But the fact is I have no suitcase."

Hilda looked coldly at Mabel for a moment. A sly smile appeared on her lips. "Mabel Hitchcock and Violet Ficher," she said, holding out the keycard.

Mabel rolled her eyes. "The name is Havelock."

"I read what is written." She gave Mabel a steely look and held up the card, waving it.

Mabel's face reddened as she snatched the keycard. She opened her mouth to reply, then feeling Violet's hand on her shoulder, she closed her mouth, steaming silently. Hilda ran hot and cold. One minute, the woman was all smiles. The next, she was downright nasty.

"Herman and Carmilla Chapman," Hilda called out.

Herman strutted up, taking the offered key. "Carmilla and I think we would rather take a day trip to one of the islands. My wife doesn't want to look at frogs."

"Frogs?" Hilda wrinkled her brow.

"The frog park. I explained to her that the park has species from all over the world. But she is not interested."

"It is not a park full of Frogs," blustered Hilda. "Did you not read anything in the brochure? Do you not know this is the famous Frogner Park? The park of the famous sculptures by Gustav Vigeland. Frogs, good God!"

An outburst of laughter from the tour passengers followed Hilda's explanation. "So, no trip to the islands?" Carmilla asked as Herman, red-faced, stomped away.

"No," snarled Herman.

Carmilla raced to keep up with her husband. The elevator door opened, and Mabel, Violet, Allan, and Bridget entered.

A flushed-faced Herman joined them. Carmilla squeezed in beside him and asked. "And no frogs hopping about?"

"The sculptures are of frogs," Herman told his wife. "Of course. I didn't mean live frogs."

Allan laughed, and Herman glowered.

Leon entered as the door began to close, his carry-on bumping Bridget as he wedged himself behind her.

Mabel turned her head in time to see the small man's hand hover over the zip on Bridget's backpack. His eyes met Mabel's; he dropped his hand and smiled. Mabel raised her eyebrows. What the heck was Leon up to?

"Is there room?" The Australian couple, Bert and Cindy, squeezed in. The door closed, and Bert pressed the button for their floor. Mabel felt claustrophobic; they were jammed in like sardines in a can. She looked worriedly up at her friend. It would be worse for Violet; she would hate being in this close contact with people. When the doors open, Violet bursts out the door. Allan and Bridget followed her. Mabel waited for Bert and Cindy as they dragged their hand luggage out of the elevator. Herman, looking at his keycard, gave Carmilla a nudge out the door.

"Wait for me," exclaimed Carmilla, pushing her way past Leon. As the elevator door began to slide shut, Leon popped out. He stumbled over Carmilla's carryall and fell against Bridget, who, in turn, bumped Carmilla. Cindy stooped to pick up the toppled bag and somehow ended up on the floor. In the ensuing commotion, Mabel's eyes narrowed as she watched Leon's hand briefly hover. Did he open the zipper on Allan's backpack as he reached down to help Cindy to her feet? Did Violet see what she saw? Was Leon a thief?

"I'm very sorry, it is my fault," Leon said.

"No worries, mate, no harm done." Cindy brushed off her jeans.

"Clumsy oaf," spat Herman.

"I'm so sorry," repeated Leon, picking up his bag and beating a hasty retreat.

Herman glared at Leon's back, then led his wife down the hallway, reiterating facts about the frog sculptures in Frogner Park.

Violet unlocked the door to their room, plopping on the nearest bed, wrinkling the white bedspread. "I'm pooped; I don't think I even want supper."

Mabel dragged her small bag in the door and dropped it on a long, narrow bench below a tall window. "You have to eat. You'll feel better once you freshen up. You shower first."

Violet sighed, straightened the bedspread, and opened her backpack, taking out the yellow plastic cylinder containing alcohol wipes. "Okay, if you're sure, I'll nip in there after I do the once over on these surfaces." She pulled out an alcohol wipe and began to clean the bedside table and the TV remote.

"I'm sure. After I shower, I'm going to wash a few things and hang them on the shower rod. I'm glad we are here for two days. Everything should be dry before we leave. I'm afraid my luggage is flying around Europe or sitting in a storage bin somewhere."

Mabel opened her little black carry-on as Violet proceeded to wipe off a long dressing table.

"What do you make of that little man, Leon?" Mabel asked, taking out her Ziplock bag containing her toothpaste and brush.

"I think he felt bad about falling over suitcases and causing a bit of a commotion."

"And I," Mabel said. "Think he may be a little light-fingered."

Violet stopped in mid-wipe and turned to face her friend. "Really? What gives you that idea?"

"I'm very observant, as you know."

Violet grinned and resumed her cleaning. "Yes, yes. What did you see?"

"First in the elevator and —" A knock at the door interrupted her. "Just a minute, and I'll tell you." Mabel crossed the carpeted room and answered the door. The porter dumped Violet's suitcase and hurried back to a luggage rack piled high with bags.

"How nice that was quick, thank you," Mabel called to the man and wheeled Violet's case into the room. "What's it like to have a suitcase with more than two days' worth of clothes."

"Never mind, I'm sure your luggage will catch up to us." Violet set her suitcase alongside Mabel's small bag. She unzipped her suitcase, taking out her toiletry bag and a bathrobe.

"I live in hope. Anyway, while you shower, I'll text my brother and see how he's making out with Mom. She is staying with him while we are on tour." She chuckled as she took her phone out of her purse. "Cyril has always been Mom's bright-eyed boy. I wonder if some of the shine has rubbed off."

# THE SUSPECTS

MABEL PULLED ON HER new white T-shirt with a picture of the Little Mermaid printed in gold. She looked at Violet, sedately dressed in a navy-blue blouse and matching slacks. "Maybe I should have purchased something a little more, well, a little more simple," fretted Mabel.

"You look fine. You're not here to impress anyone. If you like it, that is all that matters." Violet took out a white and blue scarf from her suitcase. "By the way, how is everyone back home? Is your mom okay?"

Mabel grinned. "Cyril says everything is fine, but I got the feeling he will be quite glad when Mom goes back home."

Violet chuckled and held out her scarf. "Would you like to wear my scarf? If you're worried about your T-shirt being too, um too, um sporty, this will dress it up a bit."

Mabel draped the scarf around her neck and looked in the mirror. "Yeah, I think it does help, thank you."

"You're welcome." Violet picked up her purse.

"Let's go. I'm famished. Old Hilda will be in the lobby chomping at the bit. That woman's mood changes at the drop of a hat." Mabel opened the door.

"I know; she is a little volatile."

"A little? How about a lot? And I'm in her bad books, and I don't know why." Mabel led the way to the elevator.

"Let's hope her mood has changed. I'm looking forward to supper now."

"I never told you what I saw..." Mabel's voice trailed off. Allan and Bridget were waiting at the elevator. It wouldn't do to suggest that she thought Leon had opened Allan's backpack. She might be wrong. She couldn't destroy someone's reputation on suspicion. The doors opened, and they followed the sporty-looking couple into the elevator. Leon dashed up in time to enter the elevator just as the doors began to close.

"Your vest looks so stylish, perfect for travelling," admired Mabel as Violet pressed the button for the lobby with her pen.

"We find these vests very practical when travelling," Bridget replied. She adjusted her blue-rimmed glasses with her thumb and forefinger and peered down at Mabel. "Nice T-shirt."

"Why, thank you, I bought it in Copenhagen," Mabel said, pleased with the compliment.

Allan hooted with laughter. "I think that gaudy mermaid on your shirt is a dead giveaway."

Mabel's lips tightened.

Violet turned, pen in hand, her eyes narrowed as she gave the tanned couple a sharp look. "I find jealousy as unattractive as bad manners. The golden mermaid on my friend's shirt is quite festive."

Unconcerned, Bridget ran a hand through long red locks and shrugged

"I remember you saying you travel the world," interjected Leon.

"Yes, ah, yes, we do get around," sputtered Allan.

"You've come from somewhere tropical, is my guess. You both have nice tans," Leon added.

"We have been able to travel to a great many countries, some quite warm and sunny," replied Allan as the elevator came to the main floor. Allan, Bridget and Leon stepped out, joining the others waiting in the lobby.

"Thanks, Violet, for sticking up for me. I know how you hate confrontation."

"I dislike bad manners, and better me than you."

"I guess you're right. I might have said something a little harsher."

Violet grinned. "A little?"

Mabel chuckled.

Hilda, her cheeks flushed, surrounded by the tour members, called out cheerily, "Come, come, Bjorn has the coach ready for us."

Mabel's mood lightened; Hilda was in a good mood. She decided she didn't care if people disliked her T-shirt. As Violet said, she wasn't here to impress anyone. She would enjoy her first night in Oslo.

"If you have read your brochure, you will know we are going to Holmenkollbakken, the Olympic ski hill. You are in for a treat: a beautiful Norwegian dinner. Holmenkollbakken has the most wonderful restaurant, with a spectacular view," Hilda gushed, her eyes sparkling. "And you will see the fantastic Olympic ski jump. I promise you; you won't have to jump." Hilda threw her head back, laughing heartily. Annika and the tour group joined in.

"What about allergies?" Sheila asked, peeking out from under her long bangs. "What is on the menu? I hope it's not chicken."

Hilda turned to loom over Sheila and barked. "I don't know what is on the menu. And this is a fine time to tell me you are allergic to chicken. When you signed up for this tour, you were supposed to fill out a form if you have a food allergy." Sheila took two steps back. Hilda's jaw tightened as she took her phone from her red jacket pocket. "Now, I will have to alert the restaurant to make sure there is another option for you."

"Oh, I'm not allergic to chicken; I just don't like it."

Hilda jammed the phone back into her pocket. "You dislike chicken. If the chicken is not to your liking, then perhaps you will like salad," she snapped. She turned her attention to the tour group and said, "Come, everyone, the motorcoach is waiting; hurry, hurry, don't doddle."

Pouting, Sheila followed her husband, Fred, to the bus.

The inhabitants of Oslo were out enjoying the warm evening, running and jogging. Some were dry-land cross-country skiing, skis with two rollers on mini skis with batons instead of ski poles. The passengers enjoyed a breathtaking drive up the mountain to Holmenkollbakken ski hill, where they had a spectacular view of the glistening fjords below.

"If you look. You will see many gnomes amongst the forest trees. The gnomes in Norway are symbols of good luck," Annika said, pointing out the bus window. "In the olden days, Norwegian folklore said, gnomes protected buried treasure or precious minerals. Some superstitious farmers still use them today to watch over crops and livestock."

The restaurant had the look of a ski lodge. Mabel grinned as they climbed the stairs to the deck. She'd spotted a chair made entirely from old skis. Inside, the rustic look continued with a vaulted timber ceiling. Lights hung down from chandeliers made from deer horns. The big brick fireplace gave the restaurant a cozy feel. The maître d' ushered them into a large dining room. The tables were set in front of long, wide windows, giving them a spectacular view of the valley and fjords below.

"Hilda wasn't exaggerating," Mabel said as she laid her fork on her dessert plate. "The smoked salmon and potato dumplings were fabulous. You didn't have to worry about chicken, Sheila."

Sheila pushed her dessert around on her plate. "I know, but that nasty old biddy could have been a little more gracious."

Mabel glanced through the open doorway at Hilda, having an after-dinner drink at the bar.

"I don't think she's all that old. Are you going to finish your dessert?" Fred asked his wife. "What's it called again?"

"Krumkake," supplied Violet, taking the last forkful of the delicate waffle cone with a creamy filling.

"Yes, I am going to eat my dessert. It's delicious," Carmilla said. "Take Allan's. He's out on the deck with Bridget, admiring the view with Bjorn."

Fred reached across the table and snagged Allan's krumkake.

"As soon as you finish your desserts. Please go to the coach," Annika requested. "We have a big day tomorrow."

Mabel sat beside Violet, watching everyone climb aboard the bus. Allan, Bridget, and Leon were the stragglers. Along with Sheila, stuffing the restaurant menu into her purse, she rushed to keep up.

Back at the hotel, Hilda, the first one off the bus, hurried into the foyer. Violet and Mabel waited their turn to alight from the bus. "I'm going to ask again about my suitcase and see if it has arrived," Mabel said. She crossed the lobby floor past an open doorway leading to the bar, where music was spilling out. Hilda and Leon were seated at the bar. Hilda, giggling, held up a cocktail glass and clinked glasses with Leon before drinking a deep drink.

# Chapter Seven

After a hearty breakfast, the tour group climbed on board the bus. "Good morning, everyone," Annika said, beaming brightly. "I'm afraid you will have to put up with me. Hilda is a little under the weather this morning. But there is nothing to worry about; she will be fine."

"Under the weather? More like a hangover. Our dear tour director likes her drinks," Mabel muttered to Violet as she took a seat.

Violet, tucking a lock of her red hair behind her ear, brought a finger to her lips and shook her head. The rest of the passengers settled in their seats, and Bjorn drove them through the city.

"I'd like to tell you a little bit about Oslo and its Nordic history," Annika said.

Herman raised his hand and waived it.

"Yes, Herman?"

"I know all about it. I taught Scandinavian history."

"Excellent, then you know the Swedes, Danes and the Norwegians are the Norse people from Scandinavia, better known as Vikings."

Herman raised his hand again. "The Vikings were fierce warriors, raiding and pillaging England, Ireland, and Scotland."

"And France. But our Viking ancestors were also traders and explorers." She laughed, then added, "And they did find the new world long before that chap Columbus." Annika continued to elaborate on Nordic history, finishing as the bus pulled up in front of five massive granite gates, the cast iron doors decorated in three-dimensional figures. "Welcome to Frogner Park," she said.

"You will now see the genius of Gustav Vigeland. In this park, you will find two hundred and twelve sculptures depicting human life in all its stages."

The tree line park opened onto a large green expanse of well-manicured lawns, with a variety of flower beds flanking the long boulevard. Gardeners were out in full force, trimming and pruning shrubs. Lining the boulevard granite sculptures by Gustav Vigeland. Enormous statues of naked people engaged in various pursuits, running, wrestling, dancing and holding hands.

Mabel grimaced as she paused in front of a figure that showed an adult male fighting off a horde of babies. "I find this one very disturbing."

"It's not my favourite either," Violet agreed, and they proceeded down the concourse to a raised fountain.

"This fountain, surrounded by these twenty carved trees with sculptures, shows the four stages of life," explained Annika. "And this last tree contains a skeleton, a symbol of death."

"He certainly had a story he wanted to tell," commented Mabel; stepping back, she felt dwarfed by the tall gray granite figures.

"Not all of life is pretty," Violet said, aiming her camera at the tall monolith.

The tour members gathered around Annika as the young tour guide explained the carvings they were viewing in a smooth, even tone. "This pillar is eighteen feet high. On this raised plateau, you see sculptures carved out of granite. One hundred and twelve intertwined figures in this circle depict life from childhood to death and all life in between. Now I have bored you long enough. Please explore and enjoy the park."

The tour members dispersed, going off in different directions, taking in the massive sculpture.

"Annika is a nice break from Hilda, the drill sergeant," Mabel said as she sat down by the fountain. "If only old Hilda was too sick to continue the tour. Wouldn't that be nice?"

"Let's just enjoy the day. Are you staying here? I'm going to get some more shots."

"Go ahead, I'll just sit here and enjoy the park's beauty. I'll find you." She watched Violet sped off with her camera.

"Amazing place, interesting, strange and yet beautiful," Fred said, dropping beside Mabel.

Sheila, looking out from under her long brown bangs, asked. "Where are the souvenirs? I don't see a gift shop."

Annika, passing by, paused and said, "We shall have time for you to shop at our next stop. And remember we leave in a half-hour. I'll be at the bus out front of the gate. Please don't be tardy."

"We're coming with you," Herman said. He and Carmilla followed Annika down the concourse.

"No frogs?" muttered Carmilla to her handsome husband. "You said we would see frog statues."

"No, not here. I got confused about which park. The park with the frog sculptures is in the northern area of Norway."

Mabel heard Leon chuckle. He'd stopped to take a photo with his phone. "A professor, what a joke that man is. A frog park." He laughed again and strolled off, snapping pictures as he walked.

Mabel grinned. "Leon is right. Herman said he was a professor of Scandinavian history. And he comes up with these outlandish ideas," she murmured to Violet, who had returned to take a picture of the fountain.

"But this isn't history; this is art," Violet said, pointing her camera at a row of statues. "Anyway, please stand beside this sculpture of the old woman.

"Why the old lady? What about flower beds? I think that would be a nicer picture."

"I will. First, I want a picture to show how big these sculptures are."

"Fine, me and my likeness." Mabel stood beside the figurine depicting an old woman with her hand over her mouth. She grinned mischievously and placed her hand in front of hers.

Violet snapped the picture. "Not much of a likeness. She appears to be keeping her thoughts to herself. Unlike—"

"Who me?" Mabel grinned as she followed her friend down the boulevard.

"If the shoe fits." Violet laughed, dashing off to take pictures of the flower beds boarding the walkway. She squatted, pointing her camera at fragrant lavender flowers encircling the brilliant red hydrangeas.

A gardener, a tall man in blue coveralls with a striped red and yellow scarf wrapped around his neck, approached Violet.

He had a rake in one hand and a package in the other. The man tapped Violet on the shoulder.

"Lovely flowers," Violet said, standing and putting the lens cap back on her camera.

"Here, be quick." The man thrust the package wrapped in brown paper tied with a string.

"What is this?" Violet said, accepting the small parcel and turning it in her hands.

The gardener held out his hand, a puzzled look on his face. "What is the problem? Please hurry up."

"Hurry up?" asked Violet.

"Hot day for a scarf," Bridget said, coming up behind Violet.

The gardener looked from one woman to the other, then snatched the package from Violet's hand and hurried away, disappearing behind a hedge.

"What was that all about?" Mabel asked.

"I don't have a clue. One minute, this guy is offering me a present; the next, he takes it back."

Allan raced up to stand beside them. "That's strange," he said, panting; he appeared out of breath. "Where have you been?" he asked Bridget. He looked at Violet and Mabel, then back to his wife. "I've been looking all over for you."

"Nature called, I'm sorry."

"Really!" Allan strode away.

"I said I was sorry." Bridget's long red hair swirled around her shoulders as she rushed to keep up.

# Chapter Eight

"Here are your tickets for The Viking Ship Museum. You may keep the stub as a souvenir if you like. It has a nice image of the Viking ship you are about to see," Annika said, and she handed each tour group member a bright blue ticket.

"What do you make of what happened in Frogner Park?" Mabel pocketed her ticket stub as they entered the Viking Museum.

"You mean the gardener?" Violet asked. "I wonder what he wanted to give me?"

"Yes, that was weird. And what about Bridget and Allan? I think something is going on with those two."

"Why?"

"Remember, I told you I saw Allan and Bridget at the Tivoli Gardens? And they were talking to a guy with a red and yellow scarf."

"So."

"I think I saw an exchange of a package."

"Hum, that is odd," Violet said, taking out her camera as they followed the tour group into a large room with a domed ceiling.

"Are you taking anything I'm saying seriously?"

"I am, but it could mean anything. Bridget and Allan travel a lot. That man in Copenhagen could have been someone they met from another trip."

"And the gardener with a package is wearing the exact same type of scarf. How do you explain that?"

"It's a popular scarf."

Mabel frowned, but Violet was right. Maybe that scarf was popular.

"This way, please," called Annika. They entered a well-lit, cavernous room. "This ancient Viking ship, unearthed in nineteen hundred and four, is a burial ship for some revered leader," explained Annika. "You can see the skill of the craftsmen who built it. The ship is built entirely from oak and is over twenty-one meters long and five-point-ten meters broad. The ship would have had sails, and it would have carried at least thirty oarsmen who would have been warriors as well." Annika continued her description of the history as the tour members circled and took pictures. "If you look up at the corners of this room, you will see two small platforms which will give you a better view of the interior of the ship. After you have perused the ship, please take time to view the Viking artifacts in the glass display cases."

"Gift shop. Is there a gift shop?" Sheila asked.

Annika sighed, then smiled. "Follow me."

Carmilla briefly glanced at the Viking ship, then followed Sheila and Annika.

The rest of the tour group gathered around the ship, marvelling at how the Viking sailed the sea in such a small boat, raiding countries far from the Nordic lands.

"I wonder how the Vikings found North America?" Verity asked, puzzled as she strode beside Herman.

"Not many people know that the Vikings had a very early compass," Herman explained. "They invented it. But unfortunately, during the ice age, this knowledge was lost."

Mabel grinned. Leon was right. Herman had little or no knowledge of Scandinavia.

"Ice age, compass," snorted Sam. Chuckling, members of the tour group turned away, except for Verity, who looked at Herman with admiration.

The next stop was the Kon-Tiki Museum. As they mounted the steps to the museum, Fred timidly asked, "Herman, have you heard the old quote, *Better to remain silent and be thought a fool than to speak out and remove all doubt?*"

"Oh yes, that is a quote from Shakespeare. Twelve Nights, I think it was," replied Herman.

"I believe the play you're thinking of is *Twelfth Night*. And no, I think the quote is from Abraham Lincoln," contradicted Fred.

"Oh, you are quite wrong, although the quote might be from Robbie Burns," corrected Herman.

"Forget it, Fred, he didn't get the message, and our so-called professor here, doesn't know Dick," sneered Sam.

"What do you mean, so-called? And who is Dick?" Herman looked from Sam to Fred.

Sam roared with laughter, and Fred, with a smile on his lips, shook his head.

Annika glanced back at the men and frowned. "This, gentlemen and ladies, is the famous Kon-Tiki, a balsa-wood raft. Thor Heyerdahl, a Norwegian adventurer, sailed from

# THE SUSPECTS 69

Peru to the Tuamotus Archipelago," explained Annika. "He wanted to prove how the Polynesians might have used rafts to sail from the South Asia islands to Polynesia. Thor did succeed in the journey, but his raft crashed on the reefs of Tuamotus. You may have seen the documentary about his adventure. The film won the best documentary at the Academy Awards in nineteen fifty-one. And this documentary has since been featured on TV many times."

Sheila tapped Annika on the shoulder. "Souvenirs?"

Annika took a deep breath, then smiled at Sheila. "One fun fact: the expedition had a pet parrot named Lorita."

"Gift shop?" Sheila urged. Annika shrugged and led her and Carmilla off to the souvenir shop.

"I've never heard of this Kon-Tiki thing before. Isn't it a shame the poor man was not successful?" Verity asked.

Herman, crossing his arms, began explaining his theory to her. "Let me tell you how reed rafts could sail across the open seas. This man, Thor's mistake was how he made his raft. The Polynesians used banana skins. The skins were added to the rafts, making the rafts glide effortlessly over the reefs."

Fred rolled his eyes, Bert and the other Australians snickered, and Mrs. Patel took her husband's arm, ushering him away as he giggled out loud.

"Really," gushed Verity.

Sam's small brown eyes narrowed as he watched his wife hang onto Herman's every word. "If sand was bullshit, Herman, you'd be standing in the Sahara Desert. You don't know squat," he snarled.

Herman glowered back at Sam.

"Verity, don't listen to a word that man says. Come here." He held out a meaty hand. Verity, pouting, looked sorrowfully back at Herman as she joined her husband.

Mabel grinned. Sam did have a way with words, but he was right. Herman, the professor of Scandinavian history, was full of BS. Was the man that dense? Or was he acting? Her suspicious nature surfaced. Who was Herman?

---

BACK AT THE HOTEL, Hilda took charge. "Did Annika take good care of you?" she asked.

A big round of applause from the tour group made Annika take a slight bow. There was a spring in her step as she joined Bjorn, Allan and Bridget at the elevator.

"Good, I would expect nothing less. I have trained Annika well. Now, in case some of you haven't read the schedule. I want to remind you that we leave for Stockholm in the morning. And everyone, remember you must have your baggage out in front of your sleeping rooms by six o'clock. Do this before you go to breakfast. Last time, someone was running around at the last minute." Hilda shot a piercing look at Verity. "We will not have that again. Do you understand?"

Verity shrugged, looking unapologetic.

"If your suitcase is not out in the hallway when the porters come for it. It will be left behind. And you may not see it for days."

"I haven't seen mine for days," grumbled Mabel.

"Do not interrupt, Mrs. Hitchcock. I have important information; this is not the time for your petty complaints."

## THE SUSPECTS

"My name is Havelock, as you well know. And having no luggage is not a petty complaint," snapped Mabel.

"You're overreacting. Calm down," Hilda said in a condescending tone.

"Calm down." Mabel bristled. "I'm perfectly calm. I'm stating a fact."

"I wondered why you look so scruffy," Verity said.

"Mabel is not scruffy," defended Violet. "She is very presentable."

"Peoples, peoples." Hilda clapped her hands.

The tour group was milling around the lobby, gathering in small groups and chattering amongst themselves. Leon was off in a corner, talking on his cell phone, his back turned to the tour director. Sheila, chatting with Mrs. Patel, opened her tote bag to show her purchases, a puzzle, picturing the Frogner Park fountain, and a small wooden Viking boat. Mrs. Patel, in turn, was showing Sheila a model of a medieval castle. The women were debating if it was a replica of the Kronborg Castle from Copenhagen. The young Japanese girls had their phones out texting. And the Australians were discussing where to drink and what to eat. No one was paying any attention to Hilda.

"Enough with the chatter," Hilda said, clapping her hands again. She waited until the din decreased. "Dinner is on your own this evening."

"What time is dinner?" asked Mrs. Patel.

"Whenever you want it, you are on your own," Hilda reiterated.

The group began to mutter amongst themselves. Fred spoke up and asked. "Where? Where should we go to have dinner?"

"What do you mean, where? You can eat anywhere you want. There are many restaurants around this hotel. Or you can eat here. I am not holding your hand."

Fred's sugar bowl-ears turned red, as did his face. "Anyway, I thought we were here for two days. So how come we are leaving tomorrow?"

"That is because we have been here for two days," Hilda's voice rose.

"No, we haven't. We arrived yesterday afternoon, so yesterday was not a full day," Herman disagreed.

"As usual, you are confused."

"No, I'm not," denied Herman.

"What time do we have to have our luggage out?" asked Mr. Patel.

"Good lord." Hilda's nostrils flared. "Before breakfast. I told you before breakfast. Peoples, peoples, read the schedule."

"What time is breakfast?" Fred asked timidly.

"Six o'clock," barked Hilda. "I said breakfast is at six. Is that clear enough for you?"

"No, you said to have our luggage out by six," contradicted Fred.

"Because breakfast is at six," Hilda shrieked. "Good God." She turned on her heel and stocked away into the bar.

"If Attila the Hun would just drop dead, we could have Annika as our tour guide," Mabel muttered. And Sheila giggled.

# Chapter Nine

"Welcome to Stockholm, Sweden. Stockholm encompasses fourteen islands. This beautiful city has fifty-seven bridges. And, of course, Stockholm is famous for the Nobel Prize ceremonies, which are held here every year," Hilda announced cheerfully, launching into a monologue of the history of Sweden.

"Where can we buy souvenirs?" interrupted Sheila.

With a scornful expression on her face, Hilda looked down the aisle at Sheila. "We have just arrived in Stockholm, and already, you are asking about souvenirs. But never fear. I will make sure you get your precious keepsakes."

"All I asked was if there would be souvenirs, and she bit my head off," Sheila grumbled to Fred. "I'm going to write a letter to the tour company and put in a complaint."

Stretching out his arms, Fred, yawning, asked, "What, dear?"

Sheila shook her head. "Never mind, the dragon is watching me."

Hilda's voice boomed as she tapped on her microphone. "Everyone, wake up. I am telling you interesting information that you should take note of."

Mabel jerked awake, smacking her lips, her mouth dry. Squirming in her seat, she tugged on her jeans; they'd ridden up, and her feet were numb. She wiggled her toes. Were her feet swelling? At least the underwear she'd washed last night dried with her body heat. Violet, whose head rested on her shoulder, opened her eyes and sat up. The passengers on the bus yawned and stretched, peering out the bus window. Oslo's long, picturesque drive to Stockholm had begun early in the morning. It was now evening.

"Where are we?" asked Carmilla, shifting in her seat.

Herman, his steel-rimmed glasses perched on his forehead, adjusted the glasses, answering. "Switzerland, dear."

Hilda's voice roared over the mike. "Sweden, you have arrived in the city of Stockholm, Sweden."

Herman's face reddened. "I guess I was dreaming. Yes, of course, Sweden." His nostrils flared. "One day, she'll get her comeuppance. I'll make damn sure of it," he muttered.

Mabel, now wide awake, looked out the bus window as the bus crossed one bridge after another and down the streets lined with tall, thin houses. The three and four-story houses were painted green, blue, yellow and red, some with tiny garrets on top. The bus continued over another bridge and up a steep embankment to stop at a four-story brick hotel. As the porters piled the luggage inside the hotel doors, the tour group stood obediently in the lobby. Waiting for their room keys.

Annika returned from the front desk with sheets of paper and a handful of keycards. "Dinner is on your own time," she said. "But there are many quaint little cafés in the old town just across the bridge. It is a delightful area. You will love the little shops along the cobblestone streets. And no cars to interfere with your exploring," she said. She looked at Sheila and smiled. "And souvenirs, too."

Sheila grinned happily back.

Hilda held out her hand. "Keys, give me the keys." She gave Annika a dark look as she took the keycards and the sheets of paper. "You are my apprentice. Please remember who is in charge here."

Annika's face flushed as she stepped back.

Hilda looked at her list and announced, "Allan and Bridget Hughes." Allan took his keycard and strode over to the pile of luggage.

Hilda called out. "Herman and Carmilla Chapman." She looked over at Allan as Herman received his keycard. "Hey, you. Stop right there," she hollered.

Herman gave her a startled look. "The wrong card?" he asked.

"Not you, Herman, move along. I'm talking to Mr. Hughes."

Allan, ignoring Hilda, selected his suitcase from the pile of luggage.

"Stop. Leave the suitcases for the porters."

"I'm helping the porters. These rules of yours are ridiculous. Our luggage is already here in the lobby. This will speed things up." Allan grasped the handle of his suitcase and lifted it out from amongst the other bags.

Taking a cue from Allan, the tour group swarmed the luggage pile.

"Stop right now," demanded Hilda.

The Patels separated their bags from the rest, looking triumphantly at the tour guide. Bert and two other big

Australian men handed their suitcases to their wives and continued to paw through the pack of bags.

Hilda strode to the pile of luggage and stepped in front of the stack. She spread her arms and shouted. "I said stop, stop this instant. The porters know what sleeping room to take your luggage."

"But, it takes ages until we get our suitcases," complained Verity.

"It will take you a lot longer to get to your sleeping rooms if you don't leave these bags and get your keycards."

Allan smirked at Hilda as he and Bridget pulled their bags to the elevator. The rest of the group followed Hilda and lined up, waiting.

Hilda gave Allan a dirty look in return. She waited until the couple entered the elevator and shuffled her papers. And with a sly smile on her face, she announced. "If our smart-alecks refuse to listen, be it on their own heads. If you have read your brochures, you will know this is an overnight stop."

"I read it," announced Herman.

"That's a first," Hilda said sarcastically.

Herman's eyes narrowed, and his lips tightened.

"Then you will know tomorrow evening, we will be taking a ferry across the Baltic Sea to Helsinki, Finland. It is an overnight journey. You will not have access to your luggage until we arrive at our hotel in Helsinki. So, take out what you will need for the overnight voyage, such as medication, pyjamas, and a change of clothes."

"Do we still put our luggage out in the hall before breakfast?" asked Carmilla.

"Yes, before breakfast, while you eat, Bjorn will make sure your suitcases are on the bus for the trip to the ferry," Annika replied. Hilda gave Annika a derisive look, and Annika looked down at her hands.

"When do we see our baggage?" asked Mrs. Patel.

"I said, in Helsinki, what is the matter with you." Hilda rolled her eyes and looked down at her list of names.

"Can we take our carryalls on board?" asked Sheila.

"Of course, you can. What do you think you are going to carry your belongings in? A paper bag?"

"She's only asking," snarled Fred.

"And I am only answering. Now, enough with the questions. Mrs. Hitchcock and Mrs. Ficher," Hilda called out.

As Violet retrieved the room key. Mabel pressed her lips into a thin line and sighed. It was useless to complain about the mispronunciation of her name. The woman was never going to pronounce her proper name.

"Leave your luggage for the porters," Hilda instructed Violet as she handed her the key.

"I can't leave mine for the porters. I don't have any," grumbled Mabel.

"Do not complain to me. Instead, go to the desk and see if it has arrived," snapped Hilda as she looked down on her list, calling out another name.

"What does she think I do every time we check in?" mumbled Mabel, pulling her carry-on to the elevator.

"A RED-AND-WHITE POLKA-dot shirt. Really? You seem to travel light," commented Verity to Mabel. "Oh yeah, you have misplaced your suitcase." She giggled.

"Mabel didn't misplace her luggage, and her attire is very sensible. We are not here to impress anyone," defended Violet, slowing her pace so that Mabel could keep up as they walked over the pedestrian bridge to the old town.

Mabel smiled gratefully at her friend. But what seemed so festive in the shop in Copenhagen had lost its charm. Verity looked very stylish, dressed in a white chiffon dress, stopping above her knees and showing the girl's long legs encased in elegant tights, the back seam spelling out her name. Self-consciously, Mabel tugged on the long sleeve of her shirt. The jeans that were a bit snug were now way too tight. It must be the good food, she decided. Maybe they'd see a shop in the old town, and she could buy some new clothes.

But as Verity began to wobble. Mabel decided the girl didn't look quite so stylish. Her black high heels were slipping in between the cobblestones. She was now taking baby steps to avoid falling. Her hand was firmly clasped on her burly husband's arm.

Bridget and Allan, dressed in their usual attire, khaki pants with matching vests, marched along at a good pace in sturdy walking shoes. Their footwear was more practical than Verity's high heel shoes. The click-clacking of leather sandals on the cobblestones announced Herman and Carmilla. Carmilla, puffing, tugged on her husband's arm. "Dear, do we need to be in such a hurry?" she asked.

"I was thinking we all dine together," Herman said. "Allan, do you and your lovely wife want to join us?"

Bridget gave Herman a disdainful look. "My lovely husband and I are going to explore the old town."

"Lovely husband?" murmured Herman. Carmilla grinned.

"We might catch a bite later," Allan said. The couple sped up, hurrying down the street past Fred, Sheila and Leon, who were dawdling along in front of them.

Carmilla struggled to keep up with Herman as he hurried to walk beside Sam and Verity. Beaming admiringly at Verity, he asked, "May we join you for dinner?"

Verity smiled back. Her lashes dipped. "We'd love it, wouldn't we, darling?"

Sam put a possessive arm around his wife's shoulder. "I was thinking just you and me, sweetheart. A romantic dinner for two."

"Oh my, we certainly don't want to horn in on a romantic dinner, do we, Herman?" Carmilla's voice had a sharp edge to it.

"We'd like to have dinner with you and Carmilla," Violet said.

Mabel shot Violet a disheartened look. Great, now they would spend an evening listening to Herman.

Mabel, Violet, and their dinner companions, Herman and Carmilla, trooped down steps into a small windowless café. Massive timbers lined the ceiling, and wooden trestle tables with benches lined the room. Large red lanterns hung down from the log roof, and miniature lanterns of the same colour sat on the dimly lit room's tables. A tall, blond waiter in a Viking costume took their orders. The menu offered a choice of pickled herring or meatballs and lingonberries.

True to Mabel's fears, Herman, in his most scholarly tone, droned on and on with his version of Sweden's history. She stirred the mashed potatoes and stared at the pickled herring on her plate. She should have asked for meatballs. She gazed around the restaurant. None of the other members from their tour were in the café. She hoped they found better fare. A small, round man with a shaggy brown head of hair descended the stairs. He paused, talking to a Viking server, then threaded his way around the tables, going out a small door at the back of the café. Something about the man reminded Mabel of Leon, but the lighting was poor, and she decided she was mistaken. The man's hair was different, and the man had on a short-sleeved shirt. She remembered Leon on the bridge wearing a Nordic sweater.

"I'm looking forward to going to the city hall tomorrow to see where they give out the Nobel Peace Prize," Herman said.

"The Nobel Peace Prize is awarded in Oslo," corrected Violet, pushing her lingonberries to the side of her plate.

"You are wrong. I know for an absolute fact the prize is given out at the Stockholm city hall. Hilda said so."

"No, dear, I don't think she said Peace Prize," Carmilla timidly corrected her husband.

Herman ignored his wife and shook his finger at Violet. "My dear woman, if you paid attention, you would have heard Hilda tell us Nobel Peace prizes are given out at the city hall."

Violet bristled. "Nobel Prizes for physics, chemistry, literature and medicine are awarded here. The Peace Prize is awarded in Oslo."

Mabel hid a grin as Violet pulled out a travel book from her purse. She turned to a bookmarked page and passed the

# THE SUSPECTS

book across the table to Herman. Her friend had had enough of Herman's incorrect know-it-all attitude.

"Hum. Oh, yes," Herman begrudgingly agreed.

"Look, Allan and Bridget just came in. We should invite them to sit with us," Mabel said brightly, waving. Maybe Herman would stop blathering on with his weird, skewed facts on Scandinavia if Allan and Bridget sat with them.

The couple stood on the stairs, waved back, and then did a quick turnabout back up the stairs.

"Not the friendliest people on this tour," commented Herman as he handed the book back to Violet. "They never seem to want to mix with the rest of us."

Mabel placed her napkin over her half-eaten meal. Probably because they didn't want to listen to Herman. Or were they looking for a man wearing a scarf?

# Chapter Ten

A cool mist floated over the reconstructed Viking Village.

"A Viking village? I expected more," Herman muttered as they trooped back to the bus. "I don't think Vikings lived like this."

"I thought it was wonderful, the long timber houses and thatched roofs," disagreed Mabel. "The Vikings didn't spend all of their time ransacking and looting. What did you expect to see?"

"I'm sorry the Viking village is not to your taste, Herman. But Stockholm offers more sights. Bjorn will take us to the Old Town for our walking tour. Which I'm sure you will enjoy," intervened Annika.

Mabel wished Annika would let Herman reply. He was no Scandinavian history professor, that was for sure. And the question in her mind was, why was he pretending to be one?

"It's a good thing Annika is leading the tour today. She is much more diplomatic compared to Hilda," Violet murmured.

"Yeah, if old Broom Hilda were here, she'd take a strip off Herman for complaining."

"Please don't call her that. Someone might overhear," reprimanded Violet, putting her camera into her backpack.

"Whatever. I'm just glad old Hilda is under the weather again." Mabel chuckled. "Flu generated by a bottle."

"We already toured the old town. I thought the city hall was on our tour." Allan stepped aside to let his wife board the bus before him.

"I'm sure last night everyone did not get to see all the Old Town. So yes, we will explore the Old Town, and then we will go to the city hall," Annika said.

"The city hall? Why are we going to a city hall? I thought we were going to see the royal palace," Sheila said, "that's what was in the brochure. I'm so looking forward to seeing it."

Annika smiled politely. "I'm sorry, we were informed this morning that the royal family is entertaining dignitaries. It is the official residence of the royals."

"What a rip-off. So instead of seeing a palace, we go and see a crummy city hall," complained Sheila.

"I think you will be pleasantly surprised; oh, and there is a gift shop."

"Who wants a souvenir from a city hall?" grumbled Sheila.

The bus pulled up in the city hall parking lot with the other tour buses. Bjorn opened the door and stood, waiting for the passengers to pile out. Bridget stumbled down the step, and both Bjorn and Allan reached out a hand to steady her.

Annika ushered the group to the city hall, a big red brick building with a tall spire with three golden crowns. Inside the massive structure, she guided them past the council chamber with its beamed ceiling and hanging glass chandeliers. "The beamed ceiling is a nod to our Viking ancestor's long-houses," explained Annika. "Now, this way to the Blue Hall." She led them into an immense room. "This magnificent room is where the Nobel banquet is held. Hosted by the royal family, which, of course, is by invitation only."

"It's not blue," pointed out Verity.

Annika laughed. "Well spotted. Originally, the hall was supposed to be plastered and painted blue. But the architect fell in love with the red brick, so the brick walls were left. But the name Blue Hall stuck. Come, we go up this grand staircase and across the gallery. Don't forget to look down at this beautiful room. Did I mention the pipe organ? It is the biggest pipe organ in Scandinavia."

As Mabel and Violet climbed up the curved marble staircase, Bridget ran back down. "You're going the wrong way," joked Violet.

"I left something," she called over her shoulder.

Mabel and Violet crossed the gallery and stopped to view the Blue Hall below. A tour guide dressed in a bright red and yellow Scandinavian costume led another tour group into the room. Bridget approached the woman. They shook hands and began to chat as the new tour group wandered around the room. Then the guide shook her head and spread out her hands. Bridget abruptly turned on her heel and headed back toward the stairs. Leon, standing beside the pipe organ, talking on his cell phone, drew Mabel's attention. "Leon, the straggler, is always on his phone," Mabel murmured to Violet.

"He is probably conducting business or has a family issue." Violet leaned over the railing. Leon looked up as she snapped a picture of the pipe organ. He stared for a moment up at her, then jammed his phone in his pocket, speeding up the stairs.

"I'm almost sure I saw him last night in the restaurant."

## THE SUSPECTS

"I didn't see him, but I do think something is a bit off. Just now, he gave me the strangest look."

"I saw that too. Weird, maybe Leon thought you were taking his picture and didn't like that. But if so, why?"

"Camera shy? Anyway, come on, we're missing the tour."

Mabel took one last look at Leon as he sped up the stairs to the gallery above. "Did I tell you I think I saw him try to get into Bridget's, or was it Allan's backpack?"

"Do you think he's a thief?"

"I don't know, but I'm going to keep my eye on him."

"Darn it, Mabel, just when I thought we could get through a tour without your spidey sense flaring up."

"This is the Gold Hall, the site of the Nobel Laureate Ball," Annika said. "And you can see why this fantastic room is called the Gold Hall. The walls are decorated with eighteen million gold mosaic tiles. The tiles depict Swedish history and historical sights of Stockholm." Annika turned to Sheila. "Are you still disappointed?"

"Oh, my no, this is fabulous, and you did say there was a gift shop."

## Chapter Eleven

The tour group, crushed against a wall, listened to Hilda issue instructions as passengers continued to board the ferry. Large groups of young people with backpacks, laughing and talking loudly in foreign languages, families with children large and small crowded past with luggage piled on trolleys.

Hilda smiled and joked with the tour group as she ushered them to a deck below the dining room.

Mabel decided that the day off and the rest had done their tour guide a world of good.

"When do we get our luggage?" asked Allan as the group gathered around Hilda.

"I told you. You won't see your luggage until we dock in Helsinki. You people must learn to listen." Hilda sorted through a raft of cabin keys.

"When? I don't remember you saying anything of the kind. We want our luggage," snapped Allan.

"Oh, yes, I remember now." A smug smile formed on Hilda's lips. "You disobeyed my instructions and took off with your suitcases. It pays to follow the rules, Mr. Hughes. If you had, you would know your luggage will stay on the bus until we arrive in Helsinki."

Allan and Bridget exchanged a worried look. "What if I have medication that I need in my luggage?"

Hilda's face grew grimmer. "Fine. I shall have to get Bjorn and a custodian to take you down to the vehicle parking deck." Hilda sighed. "Bjorn and the officer from the ferry will wait while you fish out your medication." She took her phone from her pocket and began to text.

"No, forget it. We don't have any medication in our bags. But, if I did—"

"But you do not," Hilda interrupted. "Now, take the keys to the cabin assigned to you. The ferry provides an *all-you-can-eat buffet*. I have reserved tables for everyone. The name of our tour is on a reserved sign placed on the tables. Do not come crying to me if someone not with our tour is sitting at our tables. Just make them leave. You are all adults."

"This will be a fun voyage. Drinks are cheap onboard. And as you will soon find, some parties go on all night," Annika said.

"I hope it is quiet on our deck," mumbled Carmilla.

"Oh, an all-night party. That sounds like fun." Verity's big blue eyes flashed happily. Sam gave his wife a sidelong glance but said nothing.

"I wonder where I can purchase a souvenir?" asked Sheila. "A little wooden carved ferry boat would be so cute."

Mabel wondered if she could buy a T-shirt. There'd been no opportunity to purchase a shirt in the Old Town.

"Enough chitchat. Listen to me; remember, when we dock in Helsinki, you will meet me right here. On this deck at this spot. Is this understood?" Hilda waited for the murmurs of yes and the nodding of heads. She gave them all a stern look, then began calling out their names, handing each couple a key to their cabin.

The tour group quickly dispersed, and Mabel followed Violet down a flight of stairs and along a corridor into their cabin.

Violet grinned as she took in the windowless cabin with two bunk beds and a small bathroom with a sink and a toilet. "This makes the riverboat we sailed down the Nile look like a luxury liner."

Mabel tossed her small black hand luggage on the bottom bunk. "But it's only overnight we can manage. I'm starved."

Violet set her bag at the foot of the bunk beds. "I'm hungry too," she said. "But first, I want to go out on the top deck. And take one last look at Stockholm. I'll meet you in the dining room."

"No, I'll come with you. My tummy can wait," Mabel said, afraid she would get lost and take a wrong turn and end up in the bowels of the boat.

The women left their cabin and joined the crowd of passengers, swarming up the steps to the next deck. They followed their fellow travellers down a corridor past a large lounge with tables and chairs ringing a dance floor; the room was crowded with people lining up at the bar. Mabel paused on the next deck and peaked into the dining room. Her tummy grumbled as the aromas of delicious-looking food filled the air. Long tables down the middle of the dining room laden with freshly baked bread, salads, fish, meat and poultry. People were lined up on both sides of the tables, filling their plates. Reluctantly, she followed Violet out onto the deck, where passengers were leaning on the railings, watching Stockholm fade into the distance. As the ferryboat sailed through the Stockholm archipelago, they could see tiny inlets and little houses with red roofs on the islands. Then, the sun began to sink on the horizon with brilliant hues that delighted Mabel and Violet.

"This is like a prairie sunset only over water, fabulous," Violet said. "I'm not even going to take a picture. It wouldn't do it justice. I'll just savour this in my memory." They stayed on deck until sunset, and they could only make out the small islands where lights from the homes twinkled in the darkness.

Back in the dining room, Mabel spied the tables with the tour reserved signs. Fred and Sheila were already tucking into their meal; the Patels joined them, their plates filled with fish and fresh vegetables. Herman and Carmilla sat at a nearby table.

Mabel sighed. No one was sitting with them, and she was hungry. "Save us a seat, please," she requested.

"Where were you?" Carmilla asked, her mouth full of food, muffled her question. "You're missing out on the buffet."

"We were on deck watching the sunset," replied Violet.

"You better hurry up. The buffet line is getting longer," Leon said, sitting down at a nearby table with Bjorn.

Leon was right; the line was long, and they were on the tail end. When it was their turn at the buffet, the fresh-baked bread was gone. And all that remained of the salads were a few leaves of limp lettuce. It was the same with the vegetables, a few carrots, and some green mush that Mabel ignored. Potatoes, meatballs and lingonberries were all that were left.

"Beggars can't be choosers," quoted Violet.

"Wonderful, more meatballs. Like we haven't seen those at every meal, and who doesn't want more lingonberries," Mabel said. When she first arrived in Scandinavia, lingonberries were an exotic fruit. But the berries were served at every lunch and supper. They had lost their charm, but she was hungry, so she scooped up a spoonful of the berries.

They arrived back at the table to find a table full of dirty dishes that Herman and Carmilla had left. Mabel began to stack their dirty dishes, and a busboy hurried over and took them away.

"I'm not too disappointed they have left," Violet said as she took a package of alcohol wipes from her pocket, wiping the table. "I feel bad about last night."

Mabel grinned. "You mean that interesting discussion about the Nobel prizes?"

"I should have let it go. But I find Herman a bit wearing."

"A bit? I think most of his views on Vikings are from a Hollywood movie. I find him annoying and odd."

Violet took a fresh wipe from her package and cleaned her hands. "He certainly is that. And speaking of oddness. Allan and Bridget have just stopped at Bjorn's table. And Allan appears angry. He is talking rapidly and waving his hands in the air."

"What's the reaction from Bjorn and Leon? Mabel asked, shifting in her seat to turn her head.

"No, don't look; we will look nosey," Violet said, giving Mabel an alcohol wipe.

Mabel grinned; they were being nosey.

"Anyway, Leon isn't there, but Bjorn is looking as angry as Allen. And now Bridget is doing the talking. And she keeps glancing our way."

"I wonder what they are saying?"

"Now Allan is shaking Bjorn's hand."

"That's odd. Why is Allan shaking hands with the bus driver he sees daily?"

"And even stranger. I believe Bjorn just slipped Allan a piece of paper or money. I'm not sure which."

Mabel was dying to have a look, but instead, she cleaned her hands with the alcohol wipe and looked steadily across the table at Violet. "A tip?"

"No one tips until the end of the tour. Besides, Bjorn gave Allan something, not the other way around."

"Where is light-fingered Leon?"

"Did Leon actually take something from the backpacks?"

"His hand was hovering over the zipper. And to be honest, I never actually saw him take anything, but you never know."

"Well, he's not stealing the silverware. He is over at the coffee urn, pouring a cup of coffee." Violet chuckled.

"What are they doing now?"

"You mean Allan and Bridget?"

"Who else were we talking about?"

"Right, Allan and Bridget, they both gave Bjorn a nod. And now they are leaving the dining room."

As Mabel ate, she mulled over what Violet related. She looked across the table at her friend and laid down her fork. "What do you think is going on?" she asked.

"I don't know, but Allan and Bridget do go off by themselves all the time." Violet dabbed her mouth with her napkin and continued. "Even Herman noticed that. Do you remember at the city hall when Bridget dashed back down the stairs to the Blue Hall?"

"Yes." Mabel nodded.

"Bridget said she forgot something, but I didn't see her pick up anything in the room. Besides, she wears that vest with all those pockets. She never ever carries a purse. She and Alan always have a backpack. And she had her backpack on her back when she went down the stairs. So, what did she forget? And what's more, I saw her shaking hands with the tour guide and talking to her. If you did forget something, why wouldn't you hurry back to listen to Annika explain something new? And why did she listen to a tour guide's explanation of something you have already seen?"

"It appears to me that you, my dear friend, are contemplating a mystery. What happened to *Promise you won't start detecting*?" quoted Mabel. There was a mischievous sparkle in her eye.

"Well, yes. I guess I did ask you to promise. But I keep thinking about that odd encounter with the gardener in Frogner Park. Bridget and Allan appeared just as the gardener handed me that package. The gardener took one look at them and ran off. I'm curious to know what was in that package. Gardeners don't run up and offer parcels wrapped in plain brown paper to tourists."

Mabel smiled. She was pleased that Violet was as curious as she was. The only thing she liked better than food was a good mystery. And Mabel prided herself on her ability to solve them. "I, too, wonder what that package was. And the gardener was wearing a red and yellow scarf. Like the guy in the Tivoli

Gardens in Copenhagen. And I'm pretty sure the guy there exchanged a package with Allan."

"Interesting. I remember you asking if I saw Allan and Bridget on our tour. I don't remember them. But it was the start of the tour, and we were all so new to each other. So, I can't be sure either way."

"I'm sure those two are up to something. An exchange of money for the goods."

"The goods?" Violet asked.

"Yes, the goods, something they're buying. Something illegal is my guess."

Violet wrinkled her brow and said, "We don't know for sure they are buying something illegal."

"Oh, it's something illegal, all right. I have an idea. You suggested Allan and Bridget knew the guy in the park. I don't think they did. I think the red and yellow scarves are a signal for them."

"You watch too many spy movies."

Mabel leaned forward, her hands clasped on the table. "Hear me out. The guy in the park and the guy in the garden. They both had an identical scarf. A coincidence? I doubt it."

"Okay, maybe."

"My theory is Allan and Bridget don't know who their contacts are. Hence the scarf. They look for a man or woman wearing a scarf. A scarf with certain colours and design."

"Okay, that's possible," Violet conceded.

"And follows if they don't know their contact, then neither does the—"

"Right. Neither does the contact. So, you think the gardener and your man in the park wouldn't know what they look like either?"

"Exactly. I think the gardener thought you were Bridget, and he thought you were his contact."

"Really? We look nothing alike."

"Maybe enough to confuse this guy. This guy has a description of whom he was supposed to meet. You and Bridget both have red hair. And you both have similar, blue-rimmed glasses. The gardener must have thought you were his contact. So, he gives you a package. Then, when Bridget appears, he doesn't know who to give it to. Or he was afraid she was a cop. At any rate, he takes back the package and hightails it out of there."

"My glasses may have a blue frame. But they have a thinner frame than Bridget's and much more stylish."

"How would he know that?"

"And my hair is an entirely different colour. Bridget's hair is almost carrot red, while mine is auburn." Violet fluffed her hair.

"Again, how would he know? I bet the man was told to find a redhead with blue-framed glasses."

"If we're right in our deduction?"

"We are right," Mabel said firmly.

"I wonder what would have happened if I had taken the package?"

"I don't know. But if you are mistaken again for Bridget, you could be caught up in something illegal."

"But I would be innocent."

"Try explaining that to a foreign policeman."

Violet bit her lip worriedly.

"We need to keep a sharp eye on Bridget and Allan. And report to the local authorities if we see anything going down."

"Going down? You sound like an American crime show detective."

"Regardless, do you have a better idea?"

"No."

"And Leon, I think he's up to something, too."

Violet frowned. "You think he is a thief?

"I'm not sure, but my spidey sense says there is something odd about him."

"What about Herman?" asked Violet. "You have your doubts about who he says he is."

"I'll be content to watch him, too, as long as I don't have to listen to him." Mabel grinned as she placed her napkin over her half-eaten food. An unappetizing film had formed over the cold berries.

Violet pushed her plate away and folded her hands. "You don't think we're becoming busybodies like Alice?" she asked.

"Alice? No way," Mabel said sharply. Alice Woodstock was the town gossip. Alice knew the skinny on almost all the residents of their hometown of Glenhaven. "We are nothing like her. We are detecting, not snooping."

"Hey, we're forgetting about Bjorn. He either exchanged a note or money. We have to keep an eye on him, too."

# Chapter Twelve

Mabel and Violet strolled down the corridor and stopped to peek in the duty-free shop. It was crowded with shoppers. Sheila, among the crowd, holding an arm full of brightly coloured gnomes, grinned happily. Fred, plodding beside her, was sullen. Mabel paused, looking at the T-shirts displayed on a rack, then at the long line in front of the cashier. "I'll look for a T-shirt in Helsinki," she said.

They continued down the passageway, stopping at the lounge, where the music was blaring. The dance floor was packed with dancers gyrating to the beat. Violet bent her head, yelling loudly over the din into Mabel's ear. "I know the music is loud, and the crowd is noisy. But I'm for having a drink. The cabin will be fine for sleeping, but I don't fancy staying in that tiny room any longer than we have to."

"I'm game. I'll go to the bar. You see if you can find us a place to sit, preferably not with Herman," Mabel shouted back over the din.

Mabel elbowed her way to the bar, ordered two beers, and forked over some krona. She had no idea what the amount was in dollars, but it seemed relatively cheap to her. Carrying the beer with two glasses turned upside down over the bottles, she skirted around the dance floor. There was a mass of the young and the old, twirling and twisting to an old Rolling Stones song belting out from the loudspeakers. Mabel spotted Violet sitting at a small table with Allan and Bridget. She squeezed in beside Violet and passed her a beer. Sam and Verity, both carrying bottles of beer, joined them. Only one chair was left at the table, so Sam sat on it, and Verity perched on his knee.

As Sam drained his bottle of beer, Verity tapped her toes to the music.

"Come on, Sammy, sweetie." Verity tugged on her husband's arm. "I want to dance."

"We tramped all over Stockholm. I'm tired. Leave me alone."

Verity sighed, her lips in a pout.

Allan took his wife's hand, and they danced their way onto the floor.

Tapping her toes to the music, Mabel sipped her beer, looking around the crowded room. Most of the tour group had either called it a night or were shopping in the gift stores. But she spotted Leon leaning against the bar, drinking a beer and chatting with Annika. Hilda and Bjorn were sitting at a small round table near the bar. The tour guide seemed in a good mood, smiling and laughing, holding up her cocktail glass; she appeared to be toasting Bjorn. He returned the gesture, but there was no answering smile on his lips. Hilda set her glass down on the small round table and took a reluctant-looking Bjorn by the arm, dragging him onto the dance floor. The music changed, but not the volume and Allan and Bridget returned to the table red-faced.

"It's too darn hot in here," complained Allan, shedding his vest and picking up his bottle of beer, downing it.

"But that was fun," Bridget said, collapsing beside him on a chair.

Verity grabbed Allan's hand. "Dance with me, Allan, please," she said, batting her long lashes at him.

Allan gave his wife an enquiring look. She shrugged, and he and Verity made their way to the dance floor.

Sam, with a brooding look on his face, watched Verity and Allan dance. Bridget appeared unconcerned as she engaged Violet in a conversation held at the top of their lungs. As Bridget leaned over the table to catch what Violet was saying, a young, tall, skinny, blond man slipped in beside Bridget and put an arm over her shoulder. His words slurred as he asked Bridget, first in Swedish, then in English, if she would like to dance.

"No, thank you," refused Bridget, shaking his arm off her shoulder.

Grinning, the boy snatched up Allan's vest, donned it, and moonwalked away from the table.

"Hey, give that back," Bridget yelled.

The gangly boy turned his head, grinning and wiggling his hips; he danced away into the circle of dancers. Bridget chased after him. Laughing, he took her in his arms and twirled her around. Bridget slapped at his hands, yelling and tugging on the vest.

Mabel, her glass halfway to her mouth, watched Allan stop dancing with Verity and elbow his way through the crowd to his wife. He shouted, yanking the vest off the fair-haired boy. The young Swede took a swing at Allan. Allan sidestepped, and the boy, missing his target, fell. Two dancers, shouting at Allan, stopped dancing to pick the young man off the floor.

The young man hollered over his shoulder in Swedish at Allan as the couple took him across the dance floor to the other side of the room. The rest of the crowd on the floor paid no attention to the brief skirmish, continuing to twist and shake to the music. Allan, putting on his vest, escorted Bridget back to the table. "What were you doing? How could you be so careless?" he shouted at her.

"You're upset because your wife dances with another man? You were dancing with my Verity," snorted Sam. Out on the dance floor, Verity swayed, swinging her hips provocatively in time to the music.

Allan took a deep breath. "Well, yes, I guess I'm jealous. I overreacted, sorry."

Bridget, a smile pasted on her face, said, "No, it's fine, dear. I didn't want to dance with that drunken little fool."

Sam hoisted his beer to his lips, his eyes never leaving Verity as she swivelled and twisted her hips, her hands held high in the air, a look of glee on her face. Mabel watched as Bjorn left Hilda and danced his way over to join Verity. Seconds behind Bjorn, Hilda zigzagged her way into the circle of dancers. She staggered into a short, dark-haired teenager; they both tumbled onto the floor. Another group of teenagers, laughing and dancing in a circle around them, jeered. Annika jumped to her feet and slipped in between the dancers to help Hilda. Draping Hilda's arm over her shoulder, Annika weaved her way back to the table.

Sam bumped Mabel's arm as he bounded to his feet, hurrying to the exit.

"Darn," Mabel muttered, setting her glass on the table, beer running down her arm. As she took a wad of tissues from her purse, wiping her arm, she spotted Leon snaking his way across the dance floor and out the door. Mabel exchanged a glance with Violet, then jumped up from her seat.

"Where are you going?" Violet asked as she caught up to Mabel.

"Tailing Leon."

"Why?"

"I don't see Bjorn. Maybe Leon and Bjorn have a clandestine meeting."

"Wild-goose chase comes to mind," Violet said. "I'll stay here and keep an eye on the odd couple."

"Good idea, but this could be something."

"I still think it's a wild goose chase. Our main suspects are here."

"You might be right, but I'm following my nose."

She followed Leon; he passed the duty-free shop and up the stairs, past the empty dining room and out onto the deck. Far off, a darkened island's small lights glimmered. Mabel paused in the shadows; it took her a moment for her eyes to adjust to the darkness. Leon was standing by the railing. She felt foolish; the man was just getting some fresh air. Violet was right. It was a wild goose chase. She turned to leave, but loud shouts and cursing brought her up short.

Sam slammed Bjorn up against the railing. Verity grabbed her husband's arm, tugging on it. Bjorn, the taller of the two, drew back his arm, taking a swing. Sam grasped the younger man's fist in his meaty hand before it could strike him. He smirked as he twisted the clenched fist, bringing Bjorn to his knees.

Bjorn cried out in pain as Sam increased the pressure. "Verity is my wife. Keep your paws off her, or you won't have any paws."

"Let him go, Sam," instructed Leon. Coming up behind the man, he placed a hand on his shoulder. The hand on Sam's shoulder seemed to calm him down. He let go of Bjorn's clenched fist and turned to face his wife.

"Sammy, sweetie, we were just talking. It was so hot in there; I just needed fresh air." Verity tugged on her husband's arm.

"To bed now," he ordered.

"Nothing happened, sweetie, I promise," Verity said in a soft, pleading voice.

"Don't talk to me. I'll let you know when I want to hear anything out of you." Sam grabbed Verity by the arm and marched her past Mabel, who made herself small in the shadows.

"It's best not to provoke Sam," Leon said, offering Bjorn a hand.

Bjorn got to his feet, rubbing his wrist, looking shamefaced. "Strong old bugger," he muttered.

"Sam was a pro wrestler."

"I wish I had known that," Bjorn said, shaking his hand. "Damn, it still hurts."

"Come on. I'll buy you a drink," Leon offered.

"Thanks, I could use one."

Mabel shrank back in the shadows. Violet was right; they were busybodies, just like Alice. Bjorn was romancing another man's wife. And Leon was just a nice guy. He had put a stop to what could have been a nasty scene.

"Having an entertaining evening, Mrs. Havelock?" Leon asked as he passed.

"Oh, ah, yeah, why yes," Mabel sputtered.

# Chapter Thirteen

Mabel and Violet joined the tour group as they trooped into the hotel, where they waited while Annika retrieved their hotel room keys. Hilda moaned, dropping onto a big leather chair.

Annika handed the list and keys to Hilda, who grimaced and pushed the list away. "It's your turn. I have a headache. Sea voyages always do this to me," she said. Laying her head back, Hilda closed her eyes.

"Are you escorting the tour to the Temppeliaukio church?" Annika asked.

Hilda groaned and placed the palms of her hands over her eyes. "You do it. It's time you earned your stripes."

Annika beamed. "Wonderful. I look forward to escorting our little family. Helsinki is a beautiful city; there is so much to see. First, we go to the Temppeliaukio Church. Because the church was built directly into solid rock, it is known as the Church of the Rock."

"Will there be a gift shop at the church?" asked Sheila.

"Good lord," snorted Hilda. "It's a church." She stood. "I'm going to my sleeping room to get rid of this headache. Do not forget to tell them the itinerary. I'll see you at dinner." She stomped off toward the bank of elevators.

"Don't worry, you will find souvenirs," Annika cheerfully assured Sheila, who, with her arms crossed, had an angry look on her face. Annika continued, "As soon as you check in your rooms and freshen up, we will meet here in the lobby, and Bjorn will take us to the Temppeliaukio Church. And please do not wait for your luggage; it will be delivered to your rooms while we are touring Helsinki."

Mabel's ears perked up, a gift shop. She really needed to buy some T-shirts. She'd almost given up any hope of receiving her luggage before the tour ended.

"Please remember this is an overnight stop. We will be leaving early in the morning. So please have your luggage out in the hallway by six o'clock. And I'm sorry, but it will be a cold breakfast."

There were moans from the tour group.

"Why a cold breakfast?" asked Bert, the Australian man.

"Unfortunately, not all staff for the dining room will be in attendance," apologized Annika. "Now, I shall read your names out." She looked down at the list of names on her sheet of paper.

"This stinks. I paid good money for this tour. I demand a hot breakfast," stormed Herman.

"Forget about the damn breakfast. I want our luggage," snapped Allan.

"The quicker we get our luggage, the sooner we can go on tour. I'm so looking forward to seeing the Church of the Rock," interjected Bridget.

"You must not wait for your suitcases. Your luggage might not be delivered before we go on our tour," reminded Annika.

"Please, please do not wait for it. Or you will miss the Helsinki tour."

"I can see the damn suitcases piled over by the lobby door. Why can't we just take it?" snarled Allan. "We did before."

"Yeah, and look at the trouble you got into with Hilda." Herman laughed scornfully.

"To hell with her." Allan turned on his heel, striding to the piled luggage.

"Oh, well, ah. Wait, wait, here is your keycard," Annika called out. Bridget took the keycard while Allan retrieved their luggage from the pile.

Annika sighed worriedly as she called out the room numbers and handed out the keycards. The tour members took their keys and rushed to the pile of suitcases, grabbing their luggage.

Annika's voice shook as she called out, "Mrs. Havelock and Mrs. Ficher."

Mabel grinned as she took the keycards. "Thank you, Annika. You pronounced my name properly."

"You are welcome, but your name is written here as Hitchcock."

"Really. How did that happen?" murmured Mabel. Her name misspelled?

As Violet followed her fellow passengers and collected her suitcase, Mabel went to the desk to inquire about her luggage. "Has a suitcase been delivered here by a courier? The tag on the bag should have my name on it," she asked, spelling her name.

"No, mam, no baggage has been delivered," the attendant behind the desk said.

"How about for Hitchcock?"

"No, sorry," was the reply.

Disappointed but not surprised, she joined Violet and the other tour members waiting for the elevator with their hand luggage and suitcases. The elevators were crammed.

Finally, after a long delay, the women were able to board an elevator, riding up to their floor with Sam and Verity. Verity, snuggling up to her husband, laid her head on his shoulder. Sam shrugged her off. Verity bit her lip, looking anxiously into her husband's stone face. Mabel, feeling the tension, was glad when they arrived at their floor.

---

THE TEMPPELIAUKIO CHURCH, carved out of solid rock, had a domed copper ceiling. The skylight surrounded by the copper bathed the church with natural light. Untouched stone rubble lined the large church walls.

"This church is frequently used for concerts because of the wonderful acoustics," explained Annika. "On the upper balcony is the organ, which has over three thousand pipes."

"Where are the souvenir shops?" asked Sheila.

Herman tapped on Annika's shoulder. "I have a bit of a problem," he said. Mabel wondered if he was going to dispute Annika's description of the organ.

"Yes, what can I help you with," Annika answered brightly.

"Carmilla has stupidly lost her visa to enter Russia. Do you think that is a problem?"

"Well, not for the rest of us," Allan sneered.

"That isn't helpful," huffed Carmilla.

"Oh, dear, this is not good. We will have to notify Hilda," Annika said worriedly, tapping on her phone.

# THE SUSPECTS

Back at the hotel, Herman and Carmilla waited nervously in the lounge.

"Hilda is on her way down to help you," Annika told the anxious couple. Turning, she clapped her hands and announced. "Hilda has instructed me to take the rest of you on our tour of Helsinki. We will now visit the Helsinki Cathedral. A beautiful white Lutheran church with a green dome. And then, my dear friends, we will tour Helsinki's famous open-air market. Back to the bus, please. Bjorn is waiting for us."

"It will be okay. Hilda will fix your visa issue," Herman told his wife. Carmilla, biting her bottom lip, watched as the tour group began to make their way to the hotel exit.

"Good, because of Carmilla. I never got a chance to buy any souvenirs at the rock church," Sheila said.

"Sorry," Carmilla murmured, wringing her hands.

Sam looked at Verity. "You go, I'm not tramping through a flea market. I'm beat; I'm not going anywhere but to the bar. There's a hockey game on. I can hear the TV from here." Verity hugged San and kissed him on the cheek. Sam sighed. "Be a good girl, and don't buy junk." He handed her a credit card, kissed her back, then strode to the bar.

"Ice hockey?" asked Bert, the tall, lanky Australian. He and another Australian man with a snow-white brush cut followed Sam.

Cindy, Bert's wife, chuckled. "I knew it was just a matter of time before Bert jammed out." Her friend grinned, checking her purse.

"Of course, it's ice hockey. What do you call it in Australia?" Sam boomed as the door to the bar swung shut behind them.

Mr. Patel looked toward the bar, then back at his wife, who shook her head. Shrugging, he followed his wife to the door.

Fred also looked longingly toward the bar, but Sheila grabbed his arm, guiding him to the exit, following Allan and Bridget.

Hilda stomped out of an elevator and marched over to Herman and Carmilla. "I cannot believe you people. Outside of losing your passport, this is absolutely the worst thing you could have done."

"Carmilla didn't do it on purpose," Herman defended.

"No, I didn't, but what are we going to do? Will I be allowed to enter Russia?"

"We are not going to do anything," snorted Hilda. "It is I who will fix this mess if I can. Come with me. First, we search through all of your luggage. Then I make a phone call to the embassy."

"Maybe I should talk to them," Herman volunteered.

"You most certainly will not. Go on the tour. Your wife and I will deal with this lost visa."

"But I should be the one who deals with the Russian Ambassador," Herman insisted.

"The Russian Ambassador," scoffed Hilda. "It will be some little civil servant who I will be dealing with. Not the Ambassador. You go. I will fix this." She looked at Herman and shook her head. "If I can."

"It's okay, dear, you go. I don't want you to miss out on the sights," Carmilla said. She bit her bottom lip and wiped a tear off her flushed cheek.

"If you're sure, dear," Herman said, giving his wife a peck on the cheek.

Carmilla sniffed. Another tear rolled down her cheek as Herman turned on his heel and trotted to the door.

Verity put her arm through Herman's. "Come on, Herman, there is nothing you can do. Our dear tour director will fix everything. There is no use you wasting this wonderful day."

Following Violet to the bus, Mabel muttered, "I feel sorry for Carmilla. Herman is such a jerk. Leaving his wife alone with Hilda, who is no doubt browbeating the poor woman."

## Chapter Fourteen

Puffing, Mabel climbed the steps up to the enormous white Helsinki Cathedral. The green-domed church, with its four colonnades, dominated the square. Twelve life-sized apostles stood on the roofline. Inside, the white continued. As Annika explained the cathedral's architecture, Mabel tilted her head, looking up at the arches, the golden chandelier and the massive pipe organ. Out of the corner of her eye, she saw Allan and Bridget slip out of the door of the church.

Mabel tugged on Violet's arm. "I'm leaving."

"Annika is still speaking."

"It's Allan and Bridget they have left. I'm going to tail them," Mabel whispered and hurried down the aisle out the door.

Pressing her lips into a disapproving line, Violet followed Mabel out of the church. They stood on the top step, watching as Allan and Bridget sped across the courtyard. A green and yellow streetcar stopped briefly, and the couple climbed on board. As Mabel hurried down the steps, the streetcar sped away.

"Forget it; they're long gone," Violet advised, joining her on the bottom step.

Panting, Mabel threw up her hands. "Damn," she said. "I wish I'd been quicker. But if I had been, they might have seen me following them."

"And what would you have done if you had seen them with some, Scarf Man? Make a citizen's arrest?"

"I don't know," confessed Mabel.

The church door opened, and the tour group spilled out.

"Please follow me. The open-air market is just a few blocks from here," Annika said.

Mabel and Violet strolled past stalls piled high with fresh fruits and vegetables, passing booths selling fresh-cut flowers and leather goods. Mabel stopped at a stall to buy two colourful T-shirts and a brightly knitted sweater. At a nearby kiosk, Sheila poured over jewelry and homemade crafts. Fred's arms were already laden with packages. At a food tent, they each bought a Finnish meat pastry. "Let's go eat on the church steps; it looks like a popular place to have lunch," suggested Mabel.

"Well, it appears the locals are doing it, so I guess it will be okay. And look, who else is sitting there sharing a sandwich?" Violet asked as they made their way toward the steps.

Herman and Verity were sitting together, and he was laughing at something Verity said. She leaned against his shoulder, and he slipped his arm around hers. Mabel shook her head. "That girl is a born flirt; she never seems to learn. I told you about Bjorn and her on the ferry. Her husband was ready to pop Bjorn. Lucky Leon was there."

Violet pursed her lips. "His poor wife is dealing with her lost visa and the Russians, not to mention Hilda, and he's out here enjoying the sights."

"Not only the sights but Verity too, by the look of it," Mabel muttered.

"Let's hope this is just a mild flirtation. I came to tour the Nordic capitals and learn about the history, not witness a soap opera."

"Herman will be sorry if Sam finds out about this."

"The girl does not live up to her name," murmured Violet.

"Her name?"

"Verity means being true."

"Cool."

"She certainly is not."

"I mean, it's cool. You know what Verity's name means. What does my name mean?" Mabel asked.

Violet grinned. "Loveable."

Mabel grinned back. "Ah-ha, my name suits me to a T."

---

THE BUS PULLED UP TO the hotel. Carmilla, waiting in the lobby, rushed up to greet her husband. "Good news," she said. "I've, well, Hilda, found my visa."

Herman strode over to his chubby wife and hugged her. "I'm so glad. Where was it?"

"In the side pocket of my purse. I don't know how I missed it."

"Ah, my silly little goose," he said, kissing her on the forehead. He looked over her head at Verity. And Verity winked back at him.

# Chapter Fifteen

As the tour bus stopped at the border crossing into Russia, Herman stood up and ran down the aisle to the front of the bus. Leaning over Hilda, he snapped a picture of the border guard approaching the bus.

"Stop that right now. Put away your camera," demanded Hilda. "You better hope the border guard has not seen you. If she has, the guards may search all of us, including our luggage. If this happens, it will put us way behind schedule. And all because of your stupidity." Her nostrils flared, and her lips tightened.

"You idiot. Are you crazy?" yelled Allan.

"It's not the cold war now." Herman laughed and snapped another picture before returning to his seat.

"Idiot," snarled Allan again.

"Herman, what were you thinking? You could get into trouble," scolded Carmilla.

"Relax, I doubt I'm going to get into trouble because of a lousy picture," scoffed Herman, chuckling.

Bjorn opened the bus door, and the guard, a tall, slender woman in uniform, entered.

"Good morning," Hilda greeted, offering her hand.

The guard paused, screwed up her mouth, she nodded briefly at Hilda. Her sharp blue eyes scanned the passengers. "You," the woman said in harsh, heavily accented English.

Everyone watched in stunned silence as she strode down the aisle to Herman and held out her hand.

Herman looked meekly up at the guard over his steel-rimmed glasses, his defiance gone.

"Your camera," commanded the woman, her eyes narrowed.

"Is there a problem?" Herman asked, smiling meekly.

"Your camera."

"Herman, do as you are asked; do not play about," instructed Hilda.

"This camera?" Herman held up his camera.

The guard snatched it out of his hand and removed the memory chip.

"My pictures," gasped Herman.

Without a word or a backward glance, the guard strode back down the aisle and stopped to stare at Hilda. "You. Control your people."

"Yes, sorry," Hilda said, her head bobbing up and down.

"Passport control now," directed the thin blonde guard.

"Yes, of course," Hilda said obediently.

The guard exited the bus without another word.

"Not exactly a friendly greeting to Russia," said Verity to her husband.

"The man is an idiot," replied Sam.

"My memory card, she took my memory card," huffed Herman.

"You're lucky that's all she did," snapped Allan.

"Do not worry," Annika said. "It was a mistake, no harm done."

Hilda, looming over Herman, said, "You, Mr. Chapman, are a very fortunate man. A tour is built on schedules. Because of your foolishness, you could have derailed this tour. Your thoughtlessness would have impacted all of your fellow travellers. I will tolerate no disobedience from now on. Do you understand me?"

Herman nodded meekly.

"Good. Off the bus, everyone, and you better all have your passports and visas ready." Hilda eyed Carmilla.

"I do, I do." Carmilla waved her visa.

Hilda turned her attention back to Herman. "Remember what I said." She turned and stomped down the steps and out the bus door.

Herman lowered his head, mumbling to his wife. "How was I to know? I hope I get my memory chip back.

"You were very foolish," Carmilla said, putting her visa into her purse.

"Do you think we can buy souvenirs here?" asked Sheila.

"Not likely; this is passport control, not a tourist shop," growled Fred, levering himself out of his seat.

Hilda stuck her head in through the bus door and shouted, "Come along, we have a schedule to keep."

The tour group filed into the building, and one by one, they handed over their visas and passports. The only one singled out for attention was Herman. Herman was taken to a small room. When he came out of the room, he smiled weakly and scurried out of the building. Outside the terminal, Bjorn stood by the cargo door as the customs officials pulled the luggage from the locker under the bus. Hilda paced beside the bus as the officers randomly selected suitcases to search.

"I bet Herman's suitcase will be given a good going over. And this delay will not improve Hilda's disposition," Mabel said to Violet as they lined up outside a small grey cinder block building that housed the washrooms.

They shuffled down the line. Then Violet stood stock still. "The men are using this toilet too. That can't be right?"

"No one else seems to mind," Mabel replied with more bravado than she felt.

Inside the building, sitting on a worn wooden stool, an old woman with a weathered face, a bright red and green babushka tied under her chin. In exchange for a few kopeks, she ripped off a few pieces of toilet tissue.

Violet and Mabel each gave her the required coins and accepted two of the rough toilet paper squares. Mabel grinned as she dug in her fanny-pack and handed Violet a handful of Kleenex. "See, I knew this would come in handy." Violet accepted the tissue and waited in line for a cubicle. The smell of many years of use greeted Mabel as she entered the long, windowless room with dirty yellow walls and cracked green tiles. Mabel stepped into the tiny stall and shut the battered door. It swung ajar, the latch broken; she sat with one foot braced against the door. Flushing the toilet, she went to a long line of old stained porcelain sinks. Each sink had one tap. Corroded faucets were trickling cold water down into chipped sinks.

Violet rushed out of her cubical. "Stand here in front of this stall. Don't let anyone in there," she instructed Mabel.

Then, without waiting for an answer, she sped to the door. She raised her hand, waving to the attendant. "Please come."

The babushka woman, frowning at Violet, continued to dole out small toilet tissue squares to the waiting tourists. Finally, in answer to Violet's urgent summons, she mumbled something in Russian, clearly not understanding a word Violet said.

"Quick, come with me, Violet yanked at her arm. The reluctant woman shrugged, left her post and followed Violet into the room with the toilet stalls.

Mabel, standing guard in front of the cubical Violet had vacated, looked puzzled at Violet and the babushka woman. "What the heck?"

"I pressed the toilet lever again and again, and nothing happens; the toilet isn't flushing," explained Violet. "It's a matter of sanitation."

Mabel rolled her eyes; the place had more problems than one wonky toilet. But she said, "I'll text on my app to explain. I have it set for the Russian translation." She texted, '*the toilet is broken; please find someone to fix it.*' She held the phone up for the babushka woman to hear.

The old woman's eyes widened, then she hesitantly stepped into the stall. She raised her eyebrows, grimacing and uttering a string of guttural words in Russian; she wrinkled her nose.

"Look, see." Violet crowded up to the old lady; reaching around the woman, she pressed on the lever, and the toilet flushed.

The Russian woman threw back her head and cackled loudly, chattering in her native tongue; she patted Violet on the arm.

"But at least my Russian translation worked," Mabel said, looking at her phone.

Annika, drying her hands on a course strip of paper towel, peaked over Mabel's shoulder. "I see what you texted. But I also overheard what your translation said. I'm afraid it said, come and see a great phenomenon." She chuckled.

Mabel frowned, then broke into gales of laughter.

Violet, red in the face, hurried past the queue of tourists waiting to use the facilities. Once outside, Violet squirted her hands with sanitizer. "Stop laughing," she railed at Mabel. "It isn't funny; she thinks I'm an idiot.

As Mabel continued to giggle. Carmilla gave them a puzzled look as she brushed past into the building.

"What's so funny?" Verity asked, sticking out her hand. "May I have some too? There is no hot water or soap at the sinks."

"Just a small joke," Mabel said, squirting sanitizer onto Verity's hand.

"Thank you," Verity said, rubbing her hands together. She made a beeline over to Herman, who was sitting on a wooden bench, his arms folded across his chest and a scowl on his face. Verity perched down beside him, putting her arm around him.

"I think something is brewing there," murmured Mabel.

"Forget the soap opera. That translator app of yours is useless. For God's sake, don't use it again. This wouldn't have happened if you'd purchased a proper app."

"It's not that bad."

"Not that bad? When has it ever translated properly?"

"Are you still upset about the toilet incident?" Mabel slipped her arm through Violet's. "Forget about it. Besides, you did that old lady a favour."

Violet's eyes narrowed as she walked alongside Mabel. "A favour?"

"Yes, a favour. Imagine how tedious and soul-sucking that job is, and that poor woman does it day after day. You gave her something to talk about, something that was out of the ordinary. She will be relating this story for years about the crazy tourist who thought a flushing toilet was a great phenomenon."

"Oh great, I'm a source of entertainment."

"She doesn't know you, and you will never see her again. It's not like you are going to invite her to your birthday party."

Violet looked skyward and shook her head. "Whatever, just don't use that stupid app again."

Mabel suppressed a grin, then looked with admiration at the Patels and the young Japanese men and women, bending and stretching; they looked so supple and graceful. She wished she was half as agile as the Patels, who she thought were about the same age as her. Over by a wall, Fred, basking in the sun, chatted to Leon. Sheila, standing nearby, pouted. Mabel could smell the smoke from the cigarette that Bert and his wife Cindy were sharing. She wrinkled her nose, sticking her phone in her pocket. Allan and Bridget stood apart, talking in hushed voices, watching as the inspectors shook hands with Hilda and Bjorn.

## Chapter Sixteen

"Wake up, wake up. We are in Saint Petersburg." Hilda's loud voice awoke the passengers. They stirred, yawning, licking their dried lips.

"Can we use the washroom? I don't think I can wait," Bert, the tall Australian with the white brush cut, called from the back of the bus.

"I'm hungry. Can we stop and grab a bite to eat?" Bert's wife, Cindy, asked.

Herman stretched, yawned, and asked, "Where are we?"

"Are we stopping at a gift shop?" asked Sheila.

"I give up," snarled Hilda. "We have arrived in beautiful Saint Petersburg, the Venice of the North. And all you people can think of is food, washrooms and gift shops. Here, you handle these blockheads." She handed the microphone to Annika and plopped down on the front seat.

"Hey, hey. That's darn right rude," thundered Bert.

"Yeah, we just asked a simple question," echoed Herman.

Accepting the mic, Annika stood with one hand braced on the back of her seat. "We're all tired," she said. "Let's not let a little misunderstanding get in the way of our next adventure. Dear guests, welcome to Saint Petersburg."

"I already told them that. Get on with it," grumbled Hilda.

## THE SUSPECTS

Although Annika smiled at Hilda, it was a smile that didn't reach her eyes. She took a big breath in, then released it. "Dear friends, Saint Petersburg —"

"Saint Petersburg is named after the Tsar Peter the Great," Herman interrupted.

"Good God," moaned Hilda. "I don't know why we bother escorting this tour. We should just hand everything over to Professor Know-it-all."

Bjorn chuckled, and most of the passengers joined in, with Hilda's laughter the loudest of all.

Carmilla's face flushed as Herman ducked his head down, his lips in a mutinous pout.

"Well, Herman," Annika said brightly. "That is a great guess. This beautiful city was founded by Tsar Peter the Great. But the city is named after the apostle Saint Peter. Petrograd means Peter's city. The city's name changed again under communist rule. Lenin renamed it Leningrad. After the fall of the Soviet Union, the city reclaimed its name of Saint Petersburg." Annika continued to relate facts of Saint Petersburg as the bus drove down the busy streets to the hotel.

Mabel gazed out the bus window, taking in the sights as Annika continued to give the history of Saint Petersburg. Squares of green grass with ornamental streetlights divided the four-lane street. The buildings, built side by side, were three to four-story- high, with beautiful facades painted in pastel blue, green, pink, and even yellow. Small individual chimneys poked out of the flat roofs. The bus took them over an ornate bridge that crossed the Neva River.

"This bridge we are crossing over is just one of the three hundred and forty-two bridges spanning the river, Neva. The

Neva River and canals are why Saint Petersburg is called the Venice of the North," Annika said, concluding her travel log as the bus pulled up to the hotel, a large three-story brick structure. The large gleaming brass doors swung open, and the uniformed porters lined up, waiting to receive the luggage.

Mabel made her usual trip to the front desk to ask about her suitcase and received the standard reply, '*No, her bag had not arrived.*' She joined her fellow tour members who were waiting for keycards to their rooms. This time, Annika gave out the room numbers and keys. With arms crossed, Hilda stood guard over the luggage, and no one ventured to retrieve their suitcases, not even Allan.

---

THE SMELL OF DAMP WOOD, fish and diesel fuel greeted Mabel as she stepped off the bus, following her fellow passengers onto the pier, where a brightly coloured yellow canal boat seamlessly docked. Men dressed in white embroidered shirts, red pants, and high-top black boots helped each member step aboard.

A big, burly man in a well-worn blue uniform with gold braiding on the sleeves greeted them. "Welcome aboard your city sightseeing cruise, Neva. I am Dimitri Semenov, your captain," he said briskly. "And this gentleman is your host and guide, Michail." The captain bowed, turned on his heel and strode off to the wheelhouse.

Michail, a stout-built man dressed in the same peasant costumes as the men who helped them, board, took a long drag on his cigarette before flicking it overboard into the canal. He grinned, revealing a mouthful of tobacco-stained teeth.

"Welcome, welcome," he greeted. "Please come this way. You may go below or sit on the top deck on our comfortable benches; our open-air seating will give you the best view of our beautiful city. Come, come. We will be casting off shortly." He waited until all of the group settled down on the wooden benches. "You have picked the best boat on the river Neva for your city tour via the river," he said, nodding to Hilda, who settled onto a bench beaming back. Michail continued in smooth, unaccented English, "I said river, but this is a canal. There are three hundred kilometres of canals and three hundred and forty-two bridges. We will pass under but a few of them."

Mabel shifted on the worn wooden bench, excited to view Saint Petersburg from the canal. Violet, sitting beside her, her camera at the ready.

"Is there a gift shop aboard this boat?" asked Sheila.

"No, sorry, madam, but later, you may sample our red caviar and vodka. And we will also have some traditional Cossack dancing."

Sheila sighed; Fred looked relieved.

The boat pulled away from the pier. It was like cruising down a river within a walled canyon. The canal was bordered on each side by four-story buildings in the same pastel colours Mabel had seen on the bus.

With one foot propped up on a bench, Michail talked into a microphone, pointing out historic buildings that lined the canal. "We are now passing the famous Hermitage Museum. It is the second-largest museum in the world. The Hermitage was once the winter palace of the Empress Catherine the Great," he explained.

Cameras clicked as they sailed down the Neva. A stiff breeze began blowing, and the passengers buttoned and zipped their jackets.

As they sailed under another bridge, Michail announced, "Dear friends, I invite you to come below and sample our famous vodka and caviar. And we have traditional Cossack music for your enjoyment." He led the way downstairs into a glass-covered area with tables lined up along the windows. Mabel noted small dishes with caviar and crackers, pieces of toast, and bottles of vodka sitting on each table.

On a small, raised platform at the back of the room sat the men who had helped them aboard. One man, tuning up a three-stringed oval-shaped banjo, grinned. Another man strummed on a triangular guitar, and the man with the button accordion shouted a Russian greeting.

"These talented musicians will now entertain you, and we have our famous Russian dancers." Michail clapped his hands. The group joined in, and the musicians began to play.

A blonde-haired girl with a gold and red beaded headdress danced onto the floor; her red decorative skirt flared out as she twirled. Entering, high-stepping in time to the music, a dark-haired man wearing a white embroidered shirt, an embellished red sash, bright blue narrow trousers, and high-top red boots joined her. The couple bowed and then began their dance.

Tapping her toes to the fast-paced folk music, Mabel munched on the red caviar and toast, sipping vodka, marvelling at the dancers' athleticism. The girl with light, intricate steps whirled and twirled as the man got impossibly low, squatting and kicking his feet up high in time to the lively music. Finishing with a flourish, they bowed to loud, appreciative applause. Then, in heavily accented English, the man invited the group's male members to try the Cossack kicks. Most of the men declined, including Fredd, Leon, and Mr. Patel. But Bert and two of his Australian friends accepted the challenge, doing mock stretches before two-stepping onto the dance floor. Three young Japanese men laughing and prodding each other joined them.

"Nothing to it," Herman said to his wife. "It's all about balance." He followed the others onto the floor.

Mabel clapped. She had to give Herman credit; he was game to try. She hoped for his sake this time that he was as good as his boast.

The tall Russian dancer bowed to each man, and with the music playing with a slow beat, he demonstrated the kicks very slowly. Each man, in turn, tried to follow suit, all failing miserably. The Japanese men laughing fell to the floor, along with Herman and the Australians, who good-naturedly accepted their failure, returning to their tables to drink a toast to the dancer, except for Herman, who stomped back to his table, muttering. "The floor is too slippery," he explained. "That's the only reason I fell."

Sam, hoisting his glass of vodka, said, "Not the expert you claimed to be, are you?"

Mabel selected another cracker, spreading caviar on the small cracker, and looked at the burly man sneering at Herman. Did Sam know about Verity's flirtation with Herman?

"At least I tried, and my dear wife was here to cheer me on. Where's yours?"

Carmilla squeezed her husband's arm and gushed, "You did well, Herman. I'm so proud of you for trying."

"It's none of your business where my wife is," grunted Sam; looking at Herman, he smirked. "But it is too bad she isn't here. I know she'd get a kick out of the way you fell on your backside."

"Your wife, where is she?" Hilda asked as she sat her empty glass on the table. "Annika, did you not take a headcount?"

"I did a count; I knew Mrs. Morgan was not coming with us."

"You must report to me when a passenger is missing."

"Verity is not missing," interrupted Sam. "She has a headache. So, I told her to stay at the hotel and rest up for tomorrow."

"And Bridget and Allan, where are they?" demanded Hilda.

Mabel exchanged a look with Violet. Were the couple off meeting another Scarf Man?

"At the last minute, they decided not to come," Annika said, looking worriedly at Hilda.

"Again, you failed to tell me. You are hopeless. The report I give to the company will not reflect well on you."

Annika bit her lip; tears welled up in her eyes.

Hilda rolled her eyes and sighed. "Never mind, go get me a drink. Remember to do your job properly if you want a recommendation from me."

# Chapter Seventeen

The early morning sun shone brightly down on the tour group as they filed out of the hotel to the waiting bus. Mabel squinted; she'd forgotten her sunglasses. Violet tugged on her arm, and they lined up behind Sam and Verity. Fred and Sheila were first in line to board the bus.

"Fred, today we are on the lookout for those cute little Russian stacking dolls and Fabergé eggs," Sheila said as she accepted a helping hand from Bjorn.

"You mean fake Fabergé eggs," Fred muttered, following his wife up the steps into the bus.

"Not fakes, dear; they are reproductions."

As Sam mounted the steps and plodded down the aisle, Mabel saw Bjorn take Verity's hand and wink at her as she stepped on board. Verity, smiling mischievously at the bus driver, held his hand a little longer than necessary.

Mabel frowned as she took her seat beside Violet. Sam had given Bjorn a warning. If this flirtation continued, those two were in for a whole lot of trouble. Sam was a jealous man.

"Bjorn," Hilda's voice was cold. "Pay attention to all of our guests." Her eyes narrowed and her cheeks flushed. The Patels are waiting to board."

Bjorn grinned back at her and extended his hand to Mrs. Patel. Hilda, her mouth set in a thin line, did not return his smile.

"Oh, oh, our bus driver better mind his p's and q's," Violet whispered to Mabel. "I don't think the tour company would be too happy to learn the bus driver is consorting with a married client."

"As in having it on with her."

"Mabel, for goodness' sake, what a thing to say."

"What? You can say consorting, but I can't say—"

"Consorting is more refined."

"Yes, Mother," Mabel quipped, grinning as the last of the passengers took their seats.

Annika picked up the microphone and glanced at Hilda. Hilda, eyeing Bjorn suspiciously, her lips turned down, nodded. "Do your job, girl, explain the tour. I doubt even one of them has read the schedule."

Annika's eyes darted between the bus driver and the tour director; she then turned to face the group. "Dear friends, we are taking a historical tour of Saint Petersburg. The first stop on our fascinating tour will be The Church of the Spilled Blood. Unfortunately, Bjorn cannot take us all the way to the church, but I promise you it is a short walk." Annika kept a running commentary as Bjorn drove down the busy city streets.

"Annika, take these people to the church. I will wait here on the bus with our driver," Hilda said, casting a steely look in Bjorn's direction. "And remember, our time is limited. Stick to the timetable. We have a tour time booked for the Hermitage."

Mabel trotted alongside Violet. As they neared the church, Mabel could see the magnificent onion-shaped spires. And the bell tower's cross with a gold-plated kingly crown. She wanted to stop and admire them, but Annika hurried them along. She was glad Violet was snapping pictures. At least they would have digital memories. She looked up at the five domes, elaborately decorated in jeweller's enamel, red and white, gold and green, blue and white: each spire, a different design and colour. Annika paused briefly to point out the Romanov's coat of arms.

"Why is this church called The Church of the Spilled Blood? It is kind of a gruesome name for a church," Verity asked. Mincing along on high heels, she clung to Sam's arm.

"Because of the Russian revolution, people died on the steps here," Herman said.

Carmill's eyes narrowed; her lips pursed as she looked at her husband, then Verity.

"Where the hell do you get your information? Comic books?" Sam asked in disgust.

Bert and the Australians who were following behind them burst out laughing.

As Herman's face turned red, Carmilla poked him with her elbow. "For God's sake, quit showing off. Can't you just stay quiet?"

"Herman, I'm afraid your source of information, wherever it is you got it from, is wrong," Annika said. She smiled kindly and continued. "Tsar Alexander the Third had this magnificent church built to commemorate his father, Tsar Alexander the Second. The Tsar was assassinated here, on the site of this church, in eighteen hundred and eighty-one. A bomb was thrown under his carriage, and he died."

"Ah-ha, the beginning of the revolution," Herman announced haughtily.

"No, the revolution was much later," Annika corrected. The tour group strolled closer to the church, and Annika continued explaining the history of the revolution. "There were two revolutions; the first was in nineteen hundred and five. But the one everyone probably knows about is the one that started in nineteen-seventeen. That was when the last Tsar, Tsar Nicholas and the Romanov Monarchy were dethroned. And the beginning of the new soviet." Annika paused in front of the massive bronze doors. "And now, dear friends, we are here at this beautiful church whose proper name is The Church of the Saviour of Spilled Blood. Quite a mouthful, is it not?" She smiled. "Once inside, you will see the magnificent church fully restored. Stalin's reign of terror included a ban on religion. During his rule, this church was a warehouse for potatoes. After the fall of communism, the repairs began. The citizens of Saint Petersburg are immensely proud of the restoration. And once inside, you will see why."

"Do we have to wear a scarf or something over our heads?" asked Mrs. Patel.

"No, this church is more of a museum, although, on some holy holidays, services are held in parts of the church."

The tour group entered the vast interior of the church. Domed ceilings, floors and walls were all highly decorated with icons. Every inch of the interior of the church is adorned with gold and lavish mosaics. Paintings of the apostles and other saints were encased in gold trim. The interior walls and floors were tiled in white, green and yellow marble and red jasper panels.

"The marble you see is a mixture of Russian, French, and Italian," explained Annika. "And the green pillars are decorated with malachite. And the blue you see is lazurite."

Mabel, awestruck, paused, taking in the décor, a stark contrast to the unadorned white churches of the Nordic countries.

"Have you enjoyed the tour of this magnificent church?" asked Annika, leading the way down the steps.

The group following her agreed as they stuffed their phones, iPads, and cameras in their pockets and bags.

Violet scurried over to take a picture of a flower seller surrounded by an elaborate display of fresh flowers. The young woman wearing a red and yellow babushka reached inside her matching padded jacket and pulled out a package. She extended her hand with the package.

Violet tentatively held out her hand to receive the small package wrapped in brown paper.

The woman shook her head. "Nyet, you first," she said.

"Excuse me, Violet," Verity said, stopping to admire the flowers. "Sammy dear," she called. "Come take a picture of me with this cute flower lady and these flowers."

The babushka woman jammed the package in her pocket, shouting, "Nyet, nyet, go, go."

Violet and Verity jumped back. "What a rude woman. I suppose I should offer to pay her for the picture," Verity grumbled. "With an attitude like that, she won't get one red ruble off of me." Tottering away on her high heels, she took Sam's arm.

Violet stuck her camera in her backpack and hurried over to Mabel, who was gazing up at the decorative onion domes. "It happened again," she whispered.

"What?"

"I almost received a package. And I'm sure the woman wanted money for it."

"A package? From who?"

"From whom."

"Violet, this isn't the time for a grammar lesson. Who wants money?"

"The flower lady. The woman selling flowers is wearing a red and yellow babushka. I think she mistook me for Bridget. Even though my hair is a much nicer shade of red, and my glasses are much more fashionable. But I guess the colour of my frames is the same."

Mabel rolled her eyes. "Yes, right. Tell me what happened."

Violet related the event ending with. "Verity came up just as I was about to take the package. She asked to have her picture taken with the woman. I think it was because of the flowers, and of course, the woman is dressed so colourfully."

"Yes, yes, then what happened."

"The woman got spooked, stuck the package back in her pocket and yelled at us. She told us to go."

"Are you nuts?" scolded Mabel. "Were you going to take that package? It could contain drugs. Or stolen diamonds or God knows what. Do you want to get arrested? Geez, Louise."

"Relax, I don't have the package, do I?"

"Thank goodness." Mabel grabbed Violet's arm, and they strolled down the sidewalk.

"Please do not doddle people," Annika urged. "We must not be late. Hilda has a tour booked for us at the famous Winter Palace."

Mabel looked over her shoulder in time to see the flower seller packing up her flowers into a wheelbarrow, glancing nervously at everyone who strolled past. Then Mabel spotted Allan and Bridget. They had paused to talk to the flower seller. But the woman, ignoring them, continued to pile her flowers in the wheelbarrow. Mabel grabbed Violet's arm and said, "Allan and Bridget are trying to talk to the flower woman, but she is having none of it."

Violet turned to look.

"Don't look; they might see you looking."

"You're looking."

"I'm peeking."

"There is very little difference between peeking and looking."

"Never mind, keep moving," Mabel said. "Oh look, I think an exchange is taking place."

Violet turned.

"No, don't look." Mabel grabbed her arm, propelling her forward.

"You said to look."

"Never mind, I'm sure there was an exchange of some kind. Shush, they're coming."

"I'm not the one talking," Violet whispered, watching Allan and Bridget sprint past.

As the tour members crossed over a small pedestrian bridge onto a sidewalk, a swarm of young men jumped out from between parked cars surrounding the group. The men shouting in Russian held up maps and guidebooks, milling through the tourists, pressing up against them, waving pamphlets in their faces.

"Nyet, nyet, go, go. Stay back, go, go, get out, get out of here!" screamed Annika. As quickly as they came, the men disappeared back onto the busy street. "Everyone, check your belongings; that was a gang of pickpockets."

Violet and Mabel, lagging behind the group, held their purses close to their bodies. Each member of the group was muttering excitedly and checking their pockets and bags.

"Bridget, check your pockets," shouted Allan.

Bridget gave a startled cry, "Oh my god, they took it."

"Those bastards," swore Allan, grabbing his wife's arm and pulling her to the side of the sidewalk.

Bridget continued to search the pockets of her vest. "It's no use. They took it." She looked with anguish at her husband.

"Those jerks stole from me too; they took my Russian rubles," exclaimed Rufus, a tall Asian man. "But it is okay. It was only a few rubles. And not my ID or credit cards. So, no worries."

"Anyone else?" asked Annika, aghast.

There were murmurs of no from the rest of the group as they hurried down the sidewalk to the waiting bus, worriedly looking at the other pedestrians as they passed.

"I am so sorry, Bridget; what did they steal from you?" Annika asked, walking alongside the distressed woman.

"Stuff, valuables, you know, stuff."

"Hilda or I will help you. We will go back to the hotel and sort this out."

The bus door opened, and Hilda hopped out. "It is about time; we have a schedule. Did you forget that?"

With a grim look on his face, Bjorn climbed out of the bus and watched the tour group gather by the open door. They were rechecking their belongings and chattering excitedly.

"Oh, Bridget, I'm sorry about what happened to you," Verity said. "But I hope this terrible incident doesn't interfere with our tour of the Hermitage Museum."

"No, we can't miss the Hermitage; it is so interesting. Let me tell you what we will be seeing." Herman pushed his glasses up on his nose and crossed his arms.

"Dear, please, I think Verity and everyone would like to see the museum for themselves." Carmilla grabbed her husband's arm, tugging him toward the steps of the bus.

"Do not worry. The rest of you can continue to the Hermitage. We will take Mr. and Mrs. Hughes back to the hotel in a taxi," assured Annika.

"No," protested Allan.

"What is going on here? Of course, we are going to the Hermitage. Get on the bus; we are holding up traffic."

As Annika explained the pickpocket attack to Hilda, the group began to troop past her onto the bus.

"Great! Now, I will have to sort this out. Bjorn, you take the rest of the group to the Hermitage. Annika, you go with them. And this time, try to keep them out of trouble. You people should be more careful? Every city has pickpockets. It is ridiculous to carry valuables with you when each hotel has a safe. What did they steal?"

"Nothing of importance," Allan said.

Puzzled, Annika turned to Bridget. "But you said they did."

"No, you misunderstood me," denied Bridget. "I was just upset. What the men took was nothing. Nothing important. I still have my credit cards. Everything is fine."

Pausing on the steps, Mabel listened to the exchange. Not important? The way Allan and Bridget acted after the thefts sure looked important.

"Really, did she misunderstand?" asked Hilda, her eyes narrowed. "Annika speaks perfect English. She may have her faults. But language is not one of them."

Annika's eyes widened, and a small smile appeared on her lips.

"Oh, they did take some rubles, but we can replace those," assured Allan.

"Nothing else, you are sure?" Hilda questioned, a skeptical look on her face.

"No, nothing else," assured Bridget, pushing past the tour guides onto the bus.

"Sorry, I'm late. I hope I'm not holding everyone up." Leon, panting, ran up to the bus.

"You are not holding us up; it is fine," greeted Annika.

"You are lucky, Mr. Peeters. You must stay with the group. Do not wander off by yourself again. I have enough to put up with. I do not want to have to send out a search party for you," admonished Hilda, mounting the steps after him.

The cathedral flower seller standing on the corner watched the bus pull away. The woman ripped the colourful babushka off her head and pressed a cell phone to her ear.

## Chapter Eighteen

"Welcome to the Hermitage. Here are your admission tickets," Annika said as they lined up to enter the museum.

Mabel didn't consider herself a fanciful person, but she could imagine Catherine the Great and her entourage in their beautiful court gowns crossing the white marble floors. Would they have admired the gold-decorated panels that ran the length of the large imposing lobby? Or were they so used to the opulence of the Winter Palace that they never gave it a second thought?

"As you probably know, the Hermitage is the former residence of the Russian Tsars. Perhaps the most notable to you would be Tsar Peter the Great. But did you know this massive museum actually has five interconnecting buildings?" asked Hilda. She glanced at Herman. "Nothing to add, my Know-it-all Professor?"

Herman opened his mouth and then closed it. With a satisfied look on her face, Hilda led them across the lobby.

Mabel gazed up in astonishment at the ornate white balconies and the white vaulted ceilings, which were decorated with gold leaf.

"There are antiquities from ancient Rome, as well as from Greece and Egypt and more," Hilda explained. "Your guide will show you paintings from the European masters, such as Tintoretto, Rembrandt, Leonardo DaVinci, to name just a few."

"There are three million works of art displayed in this museum. So, of course, we do not have time to view them all," Annika added as they paused at the bottom of a grand marble staircase.

"Do not interrupt me," Hilda reprimanded. "You are not the guide."

Annika flushed, and she shifted her feet, looking at the floor.

"If you insist on speaking, you might as well get on with it. Tell them about this vase."

Annika gulped and pointed to a gigantic vase. "This beautiful vase of jasper weighs nineteen tons. The magnificent vase is so large it had to be installed before the construction of the walls."

"The reason dear Annika has told you about this vase is that this is where we will all meet if we get separated, which can easily happen as there are three hundred and sixty-five rooms," interjected Hilda. "I will give you the time to meet here. Do not be late, or the bus will leave without you. And remember, most of these Russian taxi drivers do not speak English." The tour guide's piercing blue eyes gave each tour member a stern look. "Do you understand?" Everyone nodded. "Good. We will leave you now in the capable hands of your museum guide."

A thin, stooped woman with a mop of straw blonde hair in a bun on the top of her head approached. A black leather bag slung over her shoulders, and a headphone with a microphone attached to it swung by her side.

Hilda shook the new guide's hand. "This is Natalia. She is a knowledgeable expert on the art you are about to see."

Natalia smiled. "Thank you, Hilda," she said in a thick Russian accent. She turned to the tour group. "I have wireless headsets for all of you." Her smile faded as she became business-like, handing each tour group member a set of headphones. She then spoke into her microphone. There was confusion; some headsets were turned too high, others too low, and some were on the wrong channel. As Hilda and Annika helped each member of the group until all were satisfied they could hear their museum tour guide, Mabel fiddled with the earbuds in her ears; she did not want to admit that, although she could hear the guide, she couldn't understand what the woman was telling them. So, she signalled all was well with her wireless receiver.

"Do not forget the jasper vase," instructed Hilda one last time.

Mabel and her tour companions followed Natalia up the marble staircase and down a long, wide, white corridor that was bordered with gold leaf. They then entered a beautiful, enormous room displaying works of art by Italian Renaissance artists. The small woman walked briskly, describing the displays they passed. The group hurried to keep up as they filed through room after room of art, masterpieces from around the world. Mabel saw Allan and Bridget break away from the group. Should she follow the pair and find out what they were up to? Were they buyers of drugs or sellers? But Mabel was afraid she would get lost, so she stayed with Violet and the guide. Mabel knew the meeting place was beside the jasper vase, which was huge, but she doubted she would be able to find her way back to it.

As if reading her mind, Violet tugged on her arm. "We are not the police of the world. Forget about them and enjoy the tour."

Mabel nodded; Violet was right. What was she going to do? Tell a museum guard she thought they were smugglers?

Natalia, the Russian guide, showed the tour group a brief glimpse of the throne room, she then whisked them away to the knight's hall featuring life-sized statues of horses and riders both outfitted in armour. Hustling everyone from room to room, she ushered them down a beautiful hallway with massive white marble pillars and tall windows, the white walls decorated with more intricate gold leaf designs. Large crystal chandeliers encased in gold lit the way. Mabel was in awe.

The tour was conducted at a fast pace, and then Natalia paused and said, "Inside this large glass birdcage is the famous eighteenth-century golden peacock automaton clock. This life-sized mechanical clock was a gift to Catherine the Great from her husband, Tsar Peter III." Enclosed with the golden peacock was a cockerel, an owl, a squirrel and a dragonfly on a golden oak tree. Natalia waited for them to take pictures of the clock before ushering them to another room to view more paintings by European masters.

Natalia gave a running commentary on the paintings and sculptures. The guide was hard to understand, and the earbuds hurt Mabel's ears. So, she gave up trying to comprehend her heavily accented English and removed the headphones. Fortunately for Mabel, the pictures were labelled in Russian and English. She paused, studying a painting by Picasso titled *'Three Women.'* "It's a good thing there is a title, or I wouldn't have known what this picture portrays. I guess I'm old-fashioned. I like Gainsborough and the old masters better. What do you think?" she asked Violet. Mabel turned; she was alone.

Where was Violet? She looked left and right, trying to see over the heads of the tourists who crowded the room. Where was her group? She put on her headphones and heard static. Thinking she had the wrong channel, Mabel turned the dial. More static. Where was that vase? Which way would the guide lead them? Not back the way they came.

Feeling a wave of panic, Mabel sped down a corridor and turned left. Should she have gone, right? She rushed from room to room; the rooms were crowded with people viewing the paintings and sculptures, but not her group. Mabel felt sick to her stomach; she needed to calm down; she paused beside a statue. As she leaned against the wall near the sculpture, labelled *'The Three Graces.'* A sharp command in Russian and a not-so-gentle tap on her shoulder brought her up straight. A stern grey-haired woman dressed in a dark blue uniform shook her finger at her and pointed at the wall. Mabel couldn't understand the words but understood the meaning. Leaning on the wall in the Hermitage was forbidden. She stood, uncertain of which direction to take. *Get a hold of yourself, Mabel,* she told herself. *You've faced down killers.* She took her phone from her pocket. Should she use her translator app and ask for directions to the jasper vase? Mabel looked at the museum guard, then back at her phone. The darn thing would probably tell the guard she was planning on stealing the vase.

Instead, she texted Violet. '*I'm lost. Where are you? I'm here beside the sculpture Three Graces.*' Mabel looked at the screen and waited; she was never sure when she sent a text if anyone received it.

"They sure are strict here. I got my hands slapped, and all I did was touch a plaque."

Mabel's knees sagged in relief at the sound of a familiar voice.

Herman, looking flushed, asked. "Are you like me? I dumped the group. I could hardly understand a word the guide was saying." He looked at his watch. "How long before we have to meet at that vase thingy?"

Mabel's panic breathing lessened; she wanted to hug the man. "Do you know where the vase is?"

"Sure, no problem. If you're lost, follow me. I never get lost."

Mabel hoped this time Herman was telling the truth; he was such a big blowhard. But maybe he was good with directions. "Thank you. I am a little lost," she admitted, jamming the phone into her pocket.

As they roamed from room to room, Herman pointed out art by Tintoretto and Rafael. Expounding on the history and meaning of each painting. Mabel followed at his elbow. She didn't know if he knew what he was talking about, and she didn't care. Mabel had stopped admiring the art ages ago. She pointed to her watch. "I think we should be at the meeting place soon."

"Yeah, I guess you're right. Follow me."

Mabel did. They passed more fabulous sculptures and paintings, but she paid little attention until she realized they were back at the statues of *The Three Graces*.

"Herman, we've travelled in a circle. Are you sure you know the way? Time is running out. What if we're late and they leave without us? I don't speak Russian. How will we get back to our hotel?"

Herman laughed. "Don't worry, I speak excellent Russian."

"Good. Then please ask one of these ladies in blue uniforms the way to the jasper vase."

Herman's eyes darted to the stern-looking woman standing guard near a white marble pillar. "I don't know if she will understand me. My Russian might be a tad rusty."

"Please, just ask her."

"Well, to be honest, I forget most of the Russian I used to know. It's been a long time since I studied it."

Mabel folded her arms and looked over her granny glasses at Herman. She took a deep breath. "Herman, you don't know where the vase is. And you don't know Russian. Why do you do this? We need to find that vase, and you are not being helpful with your—" Mabel broke off mid-sentence. She'd spotted Leon down the corridor, standing by a pillar. She bet he knew the way.

Herman raised his hands, beads of sweat forming on his forehead. "Whoa, whoa, I can explain."

Mabel, ignoring Herman, jumped up and down, waving. Abruptly, she stopped and placed a hand over her mouth. Leon was talking to a man wearing a yellow and red scarf.

"For God's sake, woman, stop jumping up and down. I might be a little confused at the moment as to where the vase is.

But I'm not the liar that old bitch Hilda has branded me. And believe me, I'm going to fix her. She'll wish she never messed with me," railed Herman.

"What?" Mabel had lost track of what Herman was saying. Her eyes were focused on Leon and the Scarfed Man. Watching as they disappeared into another room.

"Hey, there you are. We should meet the rest of the gang by the jasper vase," hailed Violet. Trotting alongside her was Carmilla.

"Oh my gosh, Violet," Mabel said, hugging her friend. "You are a sight for sore eyes. Do you know the way to the vase?"

"Sure, follow me," Violet said, returning the hug. "I got your text that you were lost?"

"Darn right, I was. Where the heck were you?" Mabel asked.

"I was with Natalia, of course. I answered your text. But you never answered mine."

"I was on tour with Herman and didn't hear the text alert." Mabel pulled her phone from her pocket. "Oops, sorry, I have the darn thing on mute."

Taking hold of her husband's arm, Carmilla said, "You weren't with the group, Herman; I was afraid you were lost too."

"Me Lost? Good Lord, no, I found Mabel. I was showing her the way," disputed Herman.

Mabel opened her mouth, then closed it. What was the use? In Herman's mind, he was never lost.

"We better get a move on," cautioned Carmilla. "If we're late, Hilda will be in a bad mood."

Herman scowled. "When isn't she?"

Allan and Bridget joined them as they descended the marble steps to the tour group assembled by the jasper vase. Mabel could hear Sheila wondering if she had time to buy more souvenirs. And standing off to the side, Leon, with his phone to his ear.

There was no sign of the Scarf Man.

# Chapter Nineteen

"Welcome to The Peterhoff Palace. This is the Summer Palace of Peter the Great, also called Catherine's Palace," Annika said as she led the group up the steps to a long, blue two-story building with white pillars gilded with gold. "This is considered a modest palace. The palace was designed for the Tsars and their families to escape Saint Petersburg during the summer. Hence the name The Summer Palace. I will show you only a few of the forty private apartments designed for the Tzar's court; there are over a hundred private rooms. So, of course, we will only see a small part of this grand palace." Laughing cheerfully, she handed out entry tickets.

"Guides do not giggle," chided Hilda.

Annika pressed her lips into a tight line and continued to hand out tickets.

"Is there a gift shop?" asked Sheila.

Hilda rolled her eyes. "Do you know how privileged you are to visit this beautiful Palace? You have the chance to glimpse Russia's past, to see how the Tzars and Tzarinas lived." She sighed. But my dear woman, fret not. You will get to buy your precious knickknacks at the end of the palace tour." She turned to Anika. "Now get on with it, Annika, and make sure they do not dally. I will await you in the garden." Hilda strutted down the steps, taking a silver flask from her pocket and hoisting it. She took a drink, stuck the flask back into her pocket, and marched back up the steps. "On second thought, I will supervise you, Annika. Do a good job, and I will forgive your past transgressions."

"Transgressions? What do you mean by transgressions?"

"Annika, please do not make a scene. These dear tourists in our care want to see the Peterhoff Palace. Have you told our dear friends to stay in the corridor?" she asked sweetly.

"I was just about to."

Hilda rolled back and forth on her heels and said, "I see. Well, then, as usual, it is up to me to clarify the rules to my dear tour group."

Annika clenched her jaw, took a deep breath, and lowered her head.

"Each room has a narrow corridor roped off for tourists to walk. Please do not try to cross the barrier." Hilda looked expectantly at Annika. "Well, what are you waiting for? Get on with the tour."

"Poor Annika. What a rude woman," murmured Violet to Mabel. "I feel like giving Hilda a piece of my mind."

"No, you will only make things worse. Annika is a big girl. I think Annika is ready to draw a line. I think Broom-Hilda is going to get her comeuppance."

Violet, casting Annika a sympathetic look, said, "I guess."

Mabel, Violet and the group filed past two solemn-faced women who tore their tickets in half.

Annika took a deep breath, looked nervously at Hilda, squared her shoulders, and said, "This way to the great hall."

Mabel took hold of Violet's arm. She was not going to get lost again. They entered a dazzling room of white gold with long mirrors that reflected the light from the chandeliers.

"What are those tall blue and white ceramic-looking things against the wall?" Verity asked, her high heels clicking on the parquet floors.

"Those are ceramic wood stoves. You will see many of them throughout the palace," answered Annika. "The ceramic stoves were set close to the wall so the servants could feed wood into them from the other side."

"That's a little odd," commented a broad-shouldered Australian woman.

"This was so the Tsar and Tsarina and their court would not have to witness the stoking of the stoves," explained Annika.

"Good lord, pampered much?" muttered Mabel, holding onto Violet's arm; she followed Annika past an elaborately decorated banquet room set up as if to receive important guests. Violet shook off Mabel's hand and snapped a picture before moving on to the next room.

"This room is named The Chinese Room," explained Annika. "You can see why, as it is furnished in an Oriental design, with beautiful porcelain and lacquered panels, inlaid with mother-of-pearl." The tour continued. "Now we will pass The Arabesque Room. Note the decor. The ceilings, walls and doors are adorned in the rhythmic Arabic scrolling and interlaced designs." Violet and the group paused, taking pictures.

"Tsar Peter resided on the first floor, and Catherine and their children on the second floor," explained Annika. "And most of what you see, dear friends, has been restored, as the Summer Palace was severely damaged during the Second World War. Next, you will see the magnificently restored Amber Room with four hundred and fifty kilograms of decorated amber. When the Germans invaded the Soviet Union, the curators wanted to hide the priceless amber panels. But they were afraid the fragile amber would crack or even break if they moved it. So they wallpapered over it. Unfortunately, their subterfuge failed. The Germans knew of the Amber Room by reputation. The army disassembled the room in thirty-six hours, took all the amber away, and hid it. To this day, no one knows for sure what happened to the amber or its whereabouts. The restoration of the amber room began in nineteen seventy-nine. The room is restored from the original plans and drawings. You can now see the Amber Room exactly as it was, in all its glory. I must caution you to take no pictures. It is forbidden."

"I've never seen amber, have you?" Mabel asked Violet.

"No, I'm excited to view this historic room. Too bad I can't take pictures. I'll just have to keep it in my memory," answered Violet, lining up behind Sheila.

"Where is the gift shop? When will we be stopping? Soon, I hope," voiced Sheila as the group began to pass the roped-off Amber Room.

"Move along; you are holding up the line," Hilda urged. "You will get your precious imitation treasures made in China soon enough."

"Not that it's any of your business. But I'll have you know I don't buy junk," snarled Sheila, marching past the Amber Room. With his head down, Fred followed his wife.

The rest of the crew moved slowly past, taking in the ornate amber panels and long, thin gold-gilded mirrors with electric candles that flooded the room, illuminating the amber. The golden browns and rich reds of the intricate carvings in the amber gave off a warm glow.

As Mabel took her last step into the hallway, she heard a camera click. Followed by Hilda's outraged cry. "You idiot."

Mabel turned. Hilda had a hold of Herman's ear. Tugging him along like a naughty child who had his hand caught in the cookie jar. "You were told no pictures. Are you stupid or just plain willful?"

Herman sputtered, "Ow, what the hell do you think you are doing? Get the hell away from me." Red-faced, he pulled out of her grasp.

The tour group tittered at the spectacle.

"When we say forbidden, it means forbidden," Hilda said. "If any of the staff saw you taking pictures, my tour company could be denied privileges." Hilda turned to Annika. "You were to keep a close eye on these people. It will be on your shoulders if our company loses access to the Peterhoff Palace."

A white-faced Annika stood with her hands clenched at her side as Hilda stomped across the great hall and out the door.

"I'll deal with you later, you old hag." Herman, still flushed, shook his fist at the closed door.

Mabel and Violet drifted past the crowded gift shop, where Sheila and Fred were arguing.

"I think Fred is a little upset about his wife's treasure trove," Mabel said, following Violet out the massive door and down the grand steps.

"Yes, not a good day for some of our tour group. Namely Herman. Herman was in the wrong, but Hilda was over the top," Violet said. Stopping, she took a picture of the ornate, golden gilded gate leading to the garden. They then meandered down a gravel path lined with a multitude of brilliant flowers.

"And poor Annika, she bares the brunt of Hilda's tirade. And by the by Hilda, I am sure is a secret sipper," Mabel said, following Violet down the tree-lined path, past sculptures of Greek and Roman warriors.

"I know, I could smell alcohol on her breath; I hate to think what this trip would be like without Annika."

The women strolled around an array of water fountains, the sunlight sparkling on the spray. Mabel collapsed on a stone bench by the overhanging trees near one of the water fountains. Enjoying the peace and tranquillity of the fountains, spraying water skyward and then cascading down. Her legs were tired, and her head spun with the images of Catherine's palace. She leaned back on the bench, enjoying the warm sun on her face, taking in the fragrant roses and the piney smell of the junipers. Mabel looked at Violet, stretching out her long legs, sunning herself. She hated to intrude, but now that they were finally alone, it was a good time to tell Violet about Leon and the scarf-man at the Hermitage.

A giggle erupted from behind a nearby bush. "I love it when you do that, but we must be careful."

Mabel exchanged a glance with Violet, then looked around to see the source of the woman's voice. It sounded like Verity.

"There is no one but us. It is just you and me, babe." Mabel recognized the accent. It was Bjorn.

Hilda's head poked up from the other side of a fountain, stuffing a flask in her pocket. "Not alone as you think you are," she jeered. "You, you get back to your husband. I will deal with Romeo here."

Verity, buttoning her blouse, popped up from behind a shrub. Her cheeks flushed, and her hair in disarray. She ran toward the fountain, then abruptly stopped. "My shoes, my shoes."

Hilda bent. She came up with Verity's shoes, tossing them. The shoes fell into the fountain.

"Shit, shit," exclaimed Verity, pulling them out of the water. Shaking the shoes, she ran out the gate.

Bjorn jumped up from behind the bush, adjusting his clothes; he sped down the path to the gate. He was followed closely by Hilda. When she rounded the fountain, she stopped in front of Mabel and Violet. "Seen another sight, have you? One more intriguing item to write up in your dear diary." She snorted, plodding down the path after Bjorn.

"Soap opera time," Violet muttered, shaking her head as she stood, brushing off the seat of her pants.

"Verity better hope Hilda doesn't tell her husband. Sam is a jealous man. Bjorn was warned."

# Chapter Twenty

Annika stood at the front of the bus, facing the passengers with the mike in her hand. "I hope you enjoyed the Summer Palace. I've been here many times before, but this palace always—"

"Yes, I think you are right, Annika; our dear tour members did enjoy the palace." Hilda looked slyly at the bus driver. "And some enjoyed the garden even more." Bjorn's knuckles turned white on the steering wheel as he maneuvered the bus onto the road.

With a satisfied smile on her face, Hilda grabbed the microphone from Annika. "If you have read the itinerary. You will know you must put your luggage out tonight. Your bags will be transported to Moscow by bus by dear Bjorn, our popular bus driver." The bus swerved, and Hilda swayed. One hand on the back of the front seat, she braced herself. "I had better not fall," she warned Bjorn.

"Sorry. A cat ran out in front of the bus, and I don't want to run over a cat."

Hilda's eyes narrowed as she looked over her shoulder at the driver. "A cat?"

"Yes, a big grey one."

Hilda cast Bjorn a skeptical look. She placed a hand on his shoulder and whispered in his ear. The back of Bjorn's neck turned red, and he nodded. Hilda patted him on the shoulder and turned to face the passengers. "We will be taking the high-speed train to Moscow. You may keep your carry-on with you. We have an early checkout, so bring your small bags to breakfast. I have another bus to take us to the train station. Do not leave your hand luggage on the bus that takes us to the station. Or you will never see it again."

"I haven't even seen my suitcase," complained Mabel.

"If you labelled your luggage properly, you would have your bag," snarled Hilda, sitting back in her seat.

"That woman is a tyrant; she treats us all like imbeciles. No one ever stands up to her, including me," fumed Mabel.

Herman tapped Mabel on the shoulder. "I'll tell you why we put up with her. We are dependent on that loathsome woman. We are in a foreign country and don't know how to get to our destination."

"We have Annika," suggested Carmilla. "We could stage a revolt."

Herman curled his lip and snorted. "Ha, since when has Annika ever stood up to the witch? Never."

"Well, I've had it, no more Mrs. Nice Canadian. I'm going to let her have it with both barrels," vowed Mabel.

Sheila, sorting through her tote bag, leaned across the aisle and asked, "You have a gun?"

Violet rolled her eyes.

"Good Lord, no," Mabel said indignantly.

"Of course not." Herman scoffed. "How would she get a gun past customs?"

Sheila nodded. "Oh, right."

"But never mind," Herman continued. "When we get to Moscow. That bitch will get her comeuppance; I'll see to that. Grabbing me by the ear like a little boy is the last straw." He sank back in his seat, his arms crossed over his chest, his face white with anger.

# Chapter Twenty-One

It was late morning when Hilda set off at a brisk pace through the crowded train station. The tour members following her struggled to keep up.

"My feet hurt," complained Carmilla, limping alongside her husband. "I've got blisters."

"For God's sake, keep moving, or that old witch will leave us behind," urged Herman.

"Your feet hurt? Mine are killing me. Sammy, be a dear and pull my carry-on," Verity asked, tottering along beside him in her high-heeled shoes. "I should have worn flats."

"Fool woman," grumbled Sam, grabbing her hand luggage.

Fred was grumbling as he and Sheila struggled to keep up; each carried two shopping bags crammed full of packages and pulled their carry-on.

"I don't know why we had to let our luggage go by bus," Allan complained as they wove their way through the crowd of travellers.

"I, for one, would not want to be pulling my suitcase through this lot. How many trains leave this station? Half of Saint Petersburg appears to be travelling by train today," Mabel said, racing to keep up.

"What do you care?" asked Verity. "You only have your carry-on."

"Don't remind me." Mabel dodged around a crowd of young boys in school uniforms, hooting, laughing, chanting and singing in Russian.

Hilda halted, held up her hand, waved and shouted. "Here, here. Attention, everyone. Get on the train and do not be tardy; I have reserved this coach for our tour group. Get on, get on; the train has a schedule to keep."

Mabel sunk onto a green leatherette padded seat beside Violet. Facing them in the booth across a small table sat Herman and Carmilla. Mabel looked out the coach window as a sleek passenger train approached the station. The rest of the tour group boarded and settled down for their high-speed ride to Moscow.

Saint Petersburg gave way to the countryside; they flew by cultivated farmlands and small towns. Some villages appeared prosperous, with well-maintained houses. Other villages looked deserted, with rundown abandoned factories in a state of disrepair. A steward pushing a trolly down the aisle doled out pre-wrapped sandwiches and bottles of pop and water.

Mabel took a bite of her sandwich. The bread was dry, and the filling was a mushy mess of mayo and egg. As she wrapped it back up and opened her bottle of water, she noted Annika and Hilda in a heated discussion at the back of the coach. Annika broke off the argument and slumped into a seat, her arms crossed, with a mutinous expression on her face. Hilda took a flask from her pocket, took a drink, and recapped the flask. Then she made her way down the aisle, stopping to talk to each tour group member.

"Here comes the old bat," Herman muttered as Hilda swayed towards them. "She never apologized for grabbing my ear."

"That was so uncalled for," agreed his wife, patting his hand. "But you were told not to take pictures of the Amber Room."

Herman snatched his hand away and glowered.

"Of course, what she did grabbing your ear was terrible."

"Ha, no worries. I'm getting the last laugh."

"How are we this day? Are you still moping about your lost luggage?" Hilda asked Mabel; Hilda's speech was slurred.

"Despite having lost my suitcase, I have quite enjoyed this tour. Annika is a wonderful guide," Mabel said defiantly.

"Really? Annika? Well, I am afraid you are the last group to experience Annika's talent."

"You're not firing her!" gasped Violet.

"She can't fire anyone," snorted Herman.

"Herman, I never said I was going to fire Annika. As always, you are jumping to silly conclusions. Any theories about this high-speed train? Perhaps you know the inventor of this train personally." Hooting with laughter, she moved on.

Heads turned, Herman's face flushed, and his mouth formed a thin, tight line. His eyes narrowed as he watched Hilda continue her way down the aisle.

She paused to talk to the Australians. Mabel could hear Hilda mimicking an Australian accent.

When she left, Bert commented, "No tip for that woman."

"And I think she's drunk," Cindy added.

Hilda wove her way past the Japanese youngsters, tapping on their smartphones. She stopped to talk to Sheila and Fred.

"Well, my dear, our tour is almost complete. Have you enjoyed it?"

"Why, yes, thank you," replied Sheila, patting one of the shopping bags piled atop their carry-on bags.

"It is a good thing you have Fred here; he can describe to you the historical places you have been, and you can describe to him all the gift shops you have been to."

Sheila opened her mouth to reply, but Hilda moved to the next seat.

"How is the lovely Verity? Was not the Summer Palace wonderful?" She leaned down and tapped Sam on the shoulder. "Your wife certainly enjoyed the garden. Did you not, dear? Are your shoes dry?"

"My shoes? Yes, of course, they are dry." Verity glanced uneasily at Sam.

"And the garden, dear, you really enjoyed the garden. Didn't you?"

"Yes, very nice," Verity sputtered nervously.

Hilda tittered. "Just very nice, my dear me? He will be disappointed."

Verity's face flushed, and she looked pleadingly at Hilda.

"What? Who will be disappointed?" asked Sam.

Hilda smirked. "Why the Tzar, of course."

Sam's eyes darted between the two women.

Hilda moved on, stopping to talk to Allan and Bridget. "And you, have you enjoyed the tour?"

"Yes, we have, and we are looking forward to seeing Moscow," replied Allan.

"And meeting more new friends? You two are such a charming pair. Always striking up conversations with the locals. How many languages do you speak?"

"We try to be friendly, but I'm afraid we only speak English," replied Bridget.

"Really." Hilda raised her eyebrows.

"I, too, am looking forward to Moscow." Leon turned in his seat to address Hilda. "Visiting Red Square and Saint Basil's Cathedral, what a wonderful way to end the tour."

"Ah yes, Mr. Friendly. Sideling up to everyone on this tour. What is it about you, I wonder?"

Leon chuckled. "I do try to be friendly."

Mabel frowned. Hilda was right. Leon befriended almost everyone on the tour, but not Violet or her. Was that because they had nothing worth stealing?

# Chapter Twenty-Two

Rain pelted down as they hurried out of the busy train station and scrambled aboard the waiting bus. This time, no one cared where they sat. With a grim look on his face, Bjorn maneuvered the big tour bus into Moscow's heavy traffic.

Peering out the rain-splattered window, Mabel muttered, "Good Lord, I would never drive in Moscow. Bjorn is amazing. How does anyone find their way off this crowded street?"

"He is a terrific driver," agreed Violet. "We will have to tip him well."

Mabel nodded, then eager to see the sights of Moscow; she wiped the condensation off her window. But it was dark, and she only saw the lights from the cars and streetlights that glistened in the rain. The solid utilitarian buildings on the street they were travelling on looked only four stories high. But then, off in the distance, she saw taller, brightly lit buildings.

As Hilda texted on her cell phone, Annika picked up the microphone and began to advise them of their itinerary. "After we check into the hotel, we shall meet in the dining room on the main floor for a late supper. Tomorrow, we will go to Red Square and Saint Basil's Cathedral, and we will end with a visit to the Armoury. But first, we will tour the subway. The subway will be a surprise for some of you. The Moscow metro is the most beautiful subway in the world."

"A subway, yeah, right," Herman snorted. Carmilla put her hand on his arm, shaking her head.

Annika gave Herman a brief smile and continued. "Each of the stations is highly decorated. You may feel like you have entered a palace or a museum."

As the bus stopped in front of an imposing hotel, porters in rainwear scrambled out of a small door. The tour group hurried from the bus through the downpour of rain to the hotel's grand entrance, where a uniformed security guard with a pistol strapped to his waist stood inside the big glass doors. He opened the door and shouted out in Russian. Pulling her rain hood over her head, Hilda thrust herself forward to the front of the line and spoke rapidly in Russian to the guard. Mabel, her shoulders hunched, stood in the pouring rain with the rest of the group.

"What's the holdup?" shouted Allan, tugging up the collar of his jacket.

"For god's sake, can't we get out of this rain? I'm soaking wet," moaned Sheila. Everyone complaining and grumbling clustered together, pushing their way forward.

Allan grabbed Bridget's hand. They ran to the small doorway, trying to push their way past the porters into the lobby. Fred, Sheila and an Australian couple followed. Immediately, a security guard appeared in the doorway. The uniformed guard yelled out commands in Russian, and another tall, imposing guard in a rain-slicker emerged from the door and stood flat-footed with arms across his chest, blocking the

## THE SUSPECTS

way. His meaning was clear; no one from the tour group would get past him through the small door.

"Welcome to Moscow," Allan shouted at the guard. Bridget grabbed his arms, and they followed the crew back to stand in line.

"Damn it, we're getting soaked out here," shouted Sam, trying to press his way in through the main door.

The large guard put his hand on the but of his pistol and stepped in front of Sam, and Sam backed up.

Hilda turned. "Be patient. I'm going to sort this out. Annika, come with me." Hilda and Annika entered the hotel.

"Be patient? We're standing out here in this downpour," yelled Herman to the closed door. "I'm filing a complaint."

Wearing a blue raincoat, Bjorn pulled luggage from the undercarriage and set the bags on the wet pavement. The porters grabbed the suitcases, taking them through the small door.

Mabel shuffled from foot to foot. The rain was soaking her sweater. She shivered, looking enviously at the porters in their rain garb as they took the suitcases into the hotel. Bjorn, protected from the rain by the undercarriage door's overhang, reached inside the bus's storage for more luggage. Mabel scuttled over to the bus, looking for protection from the rain.

Bjorn slung another suitcase on the sidewalk, yelling, "Move, please. You are in the way."

"What the heck, that's my suitcase," exclaimed Mabel, peering into the dank hold.

"Your suitcase? I don't think so. Please join the others," instructed the bus driver.

"It is, it is," Mabel said; ignoring Bjorn, she clambered inside the baggage compartment, crawling toward her bag. The cargo hold floor was wet, dirty and smelled of mold.

Bjorn grabbed her ankle, yanking her back to the cargo door. Mabel slid along the muddy floor, yelling. "Hey, let go of me. That's my suitcase."

Violet and Fred ran over and bent down to look into the hold.

"Come out of there," urged Bjorn. "If it is your bag, I will get it for you, but one black suitcase looks much like another when you are standing out here in the rain."

Mabel climbed down, brushing the mucky grit off her hands and knees. "It is mine. I can see the red maple leaf tag."

Violet, leaning to look into the undercarriage, said, "That is definitely Mabel's tag."

Porters gathering around the cargo hold stomped their feet, muttering impatiently in Russian.

The main doors swung open, and Hilda emerged, yelling at the tour group. "Come in. Come and get in line. You and your suitcases have to go through the scanner."

Mumbling and grumbling, the passengers surged forward, pulling their carry-on bags to stand in the opulent hotel lobby, dripping onto the carpeted floor.

"You over there," shouted Hilda to Mabel and Violet. "Get in line."

"My bag, I want my suitcase."

"Now is no time to whine about your stupid suitcase; get in line."

"Come on," urged Violet. "We can sort this out in the lobby."

## THE SUSPECTS

Water dripping down Mabel's neck, she followed Violet into the lobby, joining the rest of the damp, disgruntled group.

"Attention, attention." Hilda clapped her hands. "You may go and get your luggage from the pile. Then, you and your luggage must be scanned. After you are screened, wait on the other side. Annika will give you your keycards, and the porters will take your luggage to your sleeping room."

As the tour members surged to the pile of suitcases, the security guard wearing a black suit with a pistol strapped to his belt uttered a sharp Russian command, which brought them up short.

Hilda strode over to the stack of luggage and exchanged words in Russian with the guard; then, she turned to the tour group. "I will read your name from your luggage tag. Then, you take your bag to the scanner. Show your passport, and then you and your suitcase will be scanned. Is that clear? And remember, wait on the other side for Annika, I repeat, wait for your keycard."

"Well, we can't get into our rooms without them. So, I guess we wait for our keycards," muttered Herman. "Idiot woman."

"Passports and scanning like at an airport? This is outrageous," groused Allan.

"Do they want tourists?" Sam snarled. "A great way to greet visitors to their country."

"We didn't have to do this in Saint Petersburg; this is absurd," Bridget grumbled.

"Do you want to be admitted to this hotel? Or do you want to be carted off to some police headquarters? It is your choice. I do not make the rules." Hilda stood with her arms across her chest, scowling.

The group quieted down, standing quietly in line; they took their bag when called and proceeded to the scanner.

"Violet Ficher," called Hilda as she looked at the tag on Violet's suitcase. Violet quickly took her luggage from the stack, then stood to one side, looking expectantly at Mabel.

Mabel shuffled from foot to foot, waiting impatiently for her name to be announced. She didn't even care if Hilda mispronounced her name. Name after name was called out, and the passengers claimed their luggage.

"Herman and Carmilla Chapman," Hilda said in a loud voice.

Mabel strode to the pile of luggage, arms on hips. She confronted Hilda. "Hey, hey. What about mine? I want my suitcase."

"You are being ridiculous. You know very well your bag is lost. You are holding everyone up. Move along."

"I will not. I saw my bag on the bus. I want my suitcase."

"Mrs. Havelock, you know you have no suitcase. All the luggage is unloaded. You are holding up the line. People want to go to their sleeping rooms."

"My suitcase is out in the cargo hold of the bus. I saw it."

"So did I," Violet said.

"Me too," Fred piped up.

Hilda, ignoring Mabel, looked at another name tag and called, "Allan and Bridget Hughes."

"Maybe you should go with Violet. You are causing a stir," advised Allan, taking his suitcase.

"I'm going back out to the bus, and if I have to haul my suitcase off the bus myself, I will. I don't know what enjoyment you get out of this, Hilda. But you will be damn sorry you messed with me."

"Stay where you are," Hilda said, a scowl on her face. She turned to Bjorn. "The bag. Go look in the cargo hold and get Mrs. Havelock's luggage."

Bjorn glared back at Mabel as he strode back out the door into the rain. Hilda continued to call out names; Mabel fumed as she waited for her suitcase. What was taking Bjorn so long?

Finally, the small door opened, and Bjorn returned dripping wet, pulling Mabel's battered black bag with the red maple leaf tag hanging off it. Dropping it at her feet, he shook his rain jacket, spraying Mabel.

"I can't believe you. Big joke hiding my suitcase on me." She couldn't bring herself to thank the bus driver. He had to be in on this despicable deception. But for the life of her, she couldn't think why he did this. Hilda, yes, she was a mean, spiteful woman. But Bjorn? She thought he was a good guy.

"I will have none of your disparaging comments," snapped Hilda. "Be happy you have your suitcase. Take it to be scanned and then leave it with the porter. Is that clear?"

"You held my luggage hostage because I insisted you call me by my proper name? You nasty old crow, I will be your worst nightmare. You had better keep looking over your shoulder because I will be there. You'll get yours if it's the last thing I do," Mabel said; grabbing her battered muddy bag, she marched over to the scanner.

# Chapter Twenty-Three

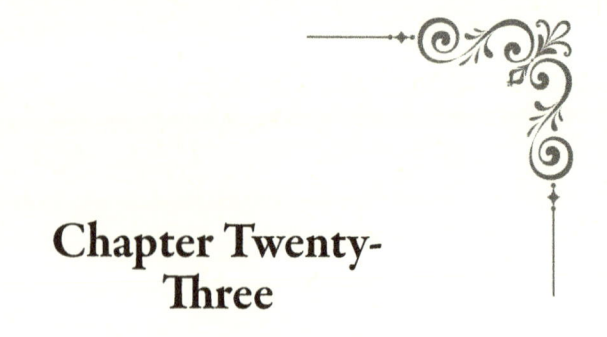

Mabel watched Violet wipe the surfaces of their hotel room with her alcohol wipes. The bright, modern room reminded Mabel of the first hotel room they stayed at in Copenhagen. The decor was grey, white and silver. Grey walls, a dark carpet in squares of different shades of grey. Two single beds, each covered with white cotton embossed bedspreads, with white padded headboards. The nightstands beside each bed held small silver lamps with white lampshades. The only splash of colour was a large picture of Red Square with Saint Basil's Cathedral in the background. Near the white-curtained windows was a long desk and a white leatherette desk chair on rollers. Sitting on the desk was a big black-screen TV. The TV looked out of place.

"I don't know who I'm madder at, Bjorn or Hilda. And how long have they been hiding my suitcase? To think, I washed out my undies and shirts nearly every night, and all the time my suitcase set in the hold on the bus," growled Mabel. She shucked off her wet sweater and pulled her suitcase across the carpet to the luggage rack.

"I know. We should report them both to the tour company."

"You darn right, I am." Mabel's lips turned down as she hoisted her suitcase and slammed it onto the luggage rack.

"Please don't let those jerks spoil Moscow for you. We only have a couple of more days on this tour." Violet unzipped her suitcase and took out a little yellow bag containing her toiletries. "This is a trip of a lifetime. Just think, tomorrow we'll see the famous Red Square, the Kremlin. And Saint Basil's Cathedral. Please, please don't let these people spoil your last days in Russia."

"Don't worry. I am determined not to let those idiots spoil Moscow for me. But I am going to report them. Thank goodness I no longer have to wear those icky clothes in my carry-on. Half the time, they were damp from washing." Mabel kicked the little bag, sending it tumbling over to the desk.

"I'm as happy as you that you have reclaimed your suitcase. I am quite sick of your gold mermaid," Violet said; taking a trip brochure from her backpack, she shook out the map. Placing it on her bed, she spread it out. "We might be able to walk to the subway tonight. Let's see how far it is from the hotel."

"I'm hungry. I'm not going out in the rain to some subway. I don't care what Annika says, '*the most beautiful subway in the world*,'" Mabel scoffed. "It's a subway. How beautiful can it be? We should shower and change for supper." She brushed at the muddy exterior of her battered suitcase. "This poor thing has been through the wars, rattling around in the luggage compartment of the bus. I almost forgot what I packed." She unzipped the bag. "Violet," Mabel shrieked. "Come look at this. This is disgusting. Someone has rifled through my clothes. Look, my clothes are messed up and crumpled."

"Good Lord. Why would someone do that?"

"More to the point, how, who, and when?" Mabel carried her suitcase to her bed and dumped out her clothes.

"This is disgraceful, most likely some overzealous customs officer." Violet rolled the desk chair to the bed and sat. "I'll help you." She shook out the wrinkles of a T-shirt, folding it neatly to the side.

"This gives me the creeps. Some weirdo pawed through my undies. Yuck."

Violet began sorting Mabel's undergarments into a pile. "Don't worry, I'll help you wash them." A small blue ticket fell onto the bed. She picked it up and turned to Mabel. "This is weird. This is the ticket for admittance to the Viking Museum."

"So, not a customs officer then."

"No, it can't be." Violet held up the ticket. "It has the image of the Viking ship on it."

"Bjorn or Hilda would be my likely suspects. Except they didn't go into the Viking Museum in Oslo with us."

"Yes, that was the morning Annika told us Hilda was under the weather."

Mabel scoffed, "The old bat was probably hung over."

"Regardless, Hilda didn't come with us to the museum. And Bjorn, of course, stayed with the bus. So he wouldn't have a ticket. So whoever rifled through your suitcase was on our tour."

A sharp rap at the door stopped Violet's reply. She strode to the door and opened it.

Hilda Karlson stood weaving in the doorway. The thickset woman put a meaty hand on the doorjamb. "I have got a. I have got. You should not..." Hilda staggered into the room past Violet, landing on the bed. The map crumpled under her weight and slid onto the carpet. She pushed herself off the bed and plopped on the desk chair. The chair spun around, rolling across the room.

Mabel and Violet exchanged an amused look as the chair wobbled in a meandering path. The woman continued to babble incoherently as the chair abruptly stopped in the bathroom doorway. Hilda became silent; she slumped forward, and her head hung down.

Violet closed the door to the hallway and grinned. "Someone has had a tad too much to drink."

Mabel stooped to pick up the map, tossing it back on the bed. "What the heck do you want? Did you come for an apology? Well, I'm not apologizing for what I said in the lobby. I meant every word. You and Bjorn should both apologize to me. And until you do. I have nothing more to say to you. So, go back to your room. You're drunk."

Hilda slumped forward in the chair and made no further comment.

Mabel and Violet exchanged a puzzled look. Violet tapped Hilda on the shoulder. "Hilda, Hilda." There was no reply. Violet looked back at Mabel. "I think she's passed out."

Mabel shrugged. "I'm not surprised. The woman was rambling; she made no sense."

"Hilda, are you alright?" Violet pulled the chair out of the bathroom doorway. Hilda's head flopped sideways.

Violet knelt, lifting the woman's head. "Oh, my gosh. Mabel, I think she's dead."

"She's passed out," snorted Mabel, crossing her arms.

Violet picked up Hilda's wrist, her fingers searching for a pulse. "No, she is definitely dead."

Mabel gently pulled Hilda upright. Hilda's dead eyes stared blankly, her mouth slack. Exchanging worried faces, the women stood looking down at the dead woman.

# Chapter Twenty-Four

Mabel bit her bottom lip, sagging onto the bed, the map crinkling under her bum. "Damn it. It's a big hotel. Why did she have to come to our room to die?"

"It doesn't matter which hotel room she picked. The poor woman is dead." Violet walked briskly to the desk and picked up the phone.

Rushing over to the desk, Mabel yanked the phone receiver out of Violet's hand, slamming it down on its cradle; she yelled, "No, stop."

Violet's eyes widened; stepping back, she put her hands on her hips. "Mabel, we must tell someone. We have to phone the front desk; they'll know what to do."

Mabel threw up her hands, waving them in the air. "The front desk? Are you nuts? This is Russia. Think about it. We are foreigners here. The Russian police will question us."

"We didn't do anything wrong. We need to report Hilda's death."

"It will look suspicious."

"Suspicious? Hilda came, and well, she just up and died."

"Exactly, she came and died. People just don't show up on your doorstep and drop dead."

"Well, she did."

"I know, and it will look suspicious."

"I repeat, we didn't do anything wrong."

"They will interrogate us. I've seen movies."

"Don't be silly." Violet reached for the phone.

Mabel looked worriedly at Violet and placed her hand over the receiver. "I'm not silly. Hilda suddenly dropped dead and in our room of all places."

"Yes, and we have to inform someone."

"They'll do an autopsy. That won't be quick."

"That's not our problem."

"Oh, but it is. We are foreigners. As I said, they'll want to question us. And there goes your Red Square, the Kremlin. Saint Basil's Cathedral. And don't forget the Cossack dancing performance. It could get even worse. We might have to stay in Moscow while they investigate. And who knows how long that will be? I want to go home. Don't you?"

"But we have to tell someone. Hilda is dead. he is here, in our hotel room." Violet bit her lips and looked across the room at the dead woman. She wrinkled her forehead and asked, "What else can we do? There is nothing for it. We have to phone the front desk."

Mabel kept her hand on the phone receiver. "We take Hilda back to her room. She's the tour director, and when she doesn't show up for the tour tomorrow morning, someone will go to her room and find her."

Violet looked sadly at Hilda. "Oh dear, I don't know."

Mabel raised her hand and placed it over her heart. "I know, I know, it sounds callous. But I mean no disrespect to Hilda. But Hilda is dead either way, here or in her own room. I, for one, do not want to be interrogated by the Russian police. Do you?"

"No." Violet slowly shook her head, looking across the room at the large woman slumped in the desk chair. "And just how do you propose we do that? We're not exactly built for lifting and carrying a dead woman."

Mabel cupped her chin, tapping her index finger on her upper lip, staring at the dead woman slumped over in the desk chair. Violet waited, nervously pacing in front of the desk, her eyes darting from Hilda to the phone.

"Aha," Mabel said. "We don't have to carry Hilda; she'll be easy to move. She's in that chair. The chair has wheels. We wheel her back to her room."

Violet raised her eyebrows. "Seriously?"

"We can do it, come on," urged Mabel, scurrying over to Hilda.

"Even if we can wheel her in that chair. How are we going to get her in her room without being seen?"

Mabel squatted down, patting Hilda's pocket, reaching into the pocket of the woman's grey cardigan. She pulled out a room keycard and read the room number. "We're in luck; her room is just three doors down. We can do this."

"Three doors down or six. We still have to get Hilda from our room to hers without being seen," worried Violet.

"No problem. We wait until everyone has gone down for supper."

"Maybe if we're lucky."

A rap on the door brought them to a standstill. "Room service," a woman's accented voice called. Violet and Mabel exchanged a horrified look.

"Just a minute, please," Mabel called back. "Oh my God, the maid,"

"I don't think room service is a maid."

"Maid, housekeeper or whatever, I don't care what she's called. We have to hide the body," hissed Mabel.

"How?" Violet hissed back.

"We put her in the bathroom, you pull, I'll push. And for God's sake, don't pull her out of the chair; we'll never get her back in."

Violet ran around the chair and took hold of Hilda's feet. Mabel grunted as they manoeuvred Hilda and the chair into the bathroom doorway. The door wouldn't close, and the back of the chair stuck out. "Pull," instructed Mabel.

"I'm standing in the tub; there's no room," Violet shouted back.

"Hush. The maid will hear you," shushed Mabel, pushing on the chair. It didn't budge. She whirled in a circle; her eyes lit on the open suitcase. She scooped up a pile of clothes off her bed, draping a sweater over Hilda's head. Then she sprinkled an assortment of clothing over the rest of the dead woman and hung a pair of slacks over the back of the chair.

"Oh, that will help. Like room service won't wonder why you have clothes hung over the chair with a dead Hilda."

"Well, you think of something then," hissed Mabel.

"We put her and the chair facing the desk."

"What if the maid notices her?"

"Like she won't notice a desk chair stuck in the bathroom doorway with clothes hung over a dead woman."

There was another rap on the door.

"Yes, yes, just a minute," yelled Mabel. "Okay," she whispered. "I'll pull on the chair you push."

"I'm not pushing on her legs."

"Don't be squeamish. Hurry up." Mabel tossed the clothes off Hilda and the chair.

"I'm not squeamish. Hilda's legs will buckle. Pull the chair, for God's sake," screeched Violet.

"Shush," Mabel muttered, tugging on the chair.

The rolled chair back out of the doorway. And Mabel parked the chair in front of the desk. Violet placed Hilda's arms on the desk and set Hilda upright in the chair.

"There," Violet said. But as soon as she took her hand away, Hilda slumped sideways. She bit her lip and looked nervously at the door.

"Room service," the voice called out loudly.

"Just a minute, please," Mabel hollered.

Violet pulled Hilda upright, but again, Hilda slumped forward.

"Hold on to her shoulders so she doesn't fall." Mabel hissed.

"That will look weird," Violet hissed back.

"If the maid sees Hilda fall over, it will look a lot weirder." Mabel hurried to the bed, grabbed the wrinkled map and spread it on the desk. "You hold Hilda's shoulder and look at the desk like she's showing you something on the map. I'll get rid of the maid; she won't suspect a thing." Kicking a sock out of the way, Mabel scurried to the door. Cautiously opening it a crack.

A tall, thin woman, her blonde hair tucked under a white and black headband, dressed in a stark white uniform, stood in the doorway. "Chocolate? Water?" she asked in heavily accented English.

"Yes, yes, that would be lovely." Mabel stood with the door slightly ajar. She glanced over her shoulder at Violet. With one hand on Hilda's shoulder, Violet's brows knitted in a worried frown, looked back.

The woman stepped into the room and handed Mabel two bottles of water. Mabel tossed the bottles onto the bed. "Chocolate, you said chocolate."

The woman reached into her apron pocket and gave Mabel two small packages of mint chocolate. "The bed, I turn for you?"

"Turn? Oh, you mean to turn down the covers on the bed. No, no, it is fine."

The maid turned toward the door.

"But more chocolate? More chocolate would be nice."

She gave Mabel a disapproving look and produced two more small packages of chocolate.

"Could I have more, please?" Mabel requested.

"Mabel," hissed Violet. "Hilda is waiting."

The woman snorted, slapping two more into Mabel's outstretched hand; she turned on her heel and went back to her cart. Mabel stood watching her wheel the cart to the next room.

She closed the door, unwrapping the tiny package of mint chocolate and popping it into her mouth. "All clear," she said.

"I can see that. Are you eating?"

"Mint chocolate. Want one?"

"How can you eat at a time like this?"

"When I get stressed, I get hungry. And I'm really stressed right now. Besides, now we'll probably miss supper."

Violet rolled her eyes. "Whatever. Now what? That woman is out there in the hallway delivering chocolate to every room."

Mabel unwrapped another mint, popping it into her mouth. "When she turns the corner at the end of the hallway, we make a break for it."

Violet strode to the door; opening it, she looked out and then closed it quickly. "She's still out there."

Mabel sat on her bed, moving the water bottles to the side table. "We wait," she said, unwrapping another chocolate wafer. "You sure you don't want one?"

"No, thanks. I think this is a bad idea. We can still phone the front desk. Maybe the police won't be as gung-ho as you think. After all, we are guests in their country."

"Yeah, right, in your dreams. Besides, room service was just here. What do we tell them? We hid Hilda because we didn't want to scare her?"

"She doesn't know we hid Hilda. And we really didn't hide her. Hilda was sitting at the desk."

"Yeah, sitting at the desk dead. It won't look good. You say guests, I say foreigners, I don't want to take a chance." Mabel went to the door and peeked out. "Come on, hurry up; the maid is gone." She pulled the door wide open, propping it with a shoe.

Violet pushed on the chair. The chair twisted to one side. Hilda's feet were trapping the wheels from moving. Violet flashed a worried look at Mabel. "Okay, Brainiac, what now? I can't move her."

Mabel backed up to the chair, picking up Hilda's ankles. With a foot in each hand, she said, "You push, and I'll pull. And don't forget to kick that shoe out of the way after we're out."

Mabel held onto Hilda's ankles as if she was pulling a rickshaw. Violet followed, pushing on the back of the chair and kicking the shoe out of the way. The door closed, and they trundled down the hallway. As Mabel tugged, Hilda began to slide off the chair.

"Stop," cried Violet in a loud whisper. "You're going to pull her out of the chair. For God's sake, just carry her feet."

They proceeded down the hallway to Hilda's room. Mabel produced the keycard and opened the door. Violet gave one last push, and they were in Hilda's room. Violet sagged on the bed as Mabel skirted around Hilda and the chair. She closed the door and flipped on the light switch. The room was a carbon copy of their room, with light grey walls and white trim. On the bedside table was a glass and a bottle. Near the open green bottle was an unopened bottle of water, and a chocolate wafer package was resting on the pillow.

"Now what? We can't leave her in this chair." Violet looked worriedly at the dead woman.

"We push the chair closer to the bed; maybe we can lever her onto it." Mabel picked the chocolate wafer package off the pillow and stuck it in her pocket.

They turned the chair until it faced the bed. Hilda drooped forward. "No, she's too heavy," moaned Violet. "We won't be able to lift her."

"Then we turn the chair. If we lift on the sides of the chair, we can dump Hilda onto the bed."

They turned the chair, each grabbed a side and strained to lift it. But it was to no avail. The chair was too heavy, and they sagged onto the bed, staring at the dead woman.

"Now what?"

Mabel opened the chocolate package and popped it into her mouth.

"Well?" Violet asked.

"We turn the chair back to face the bed."

"We tried that."

"This time, I'll stand on the bed and pull. You push," directed Mabel. "We can do this."

Mabel stood on the bed, slipping on the silky bedspread; she jumped off the bed and ripped the spread off, throwing it to the floor. She climbed back upon the bed, grasped Hilda's arms, and tugged. Hilda fell face forward onto the bed.

"Oh, poor Hilda, what are we doing?" moaned Violet.

"Never mind, we're committed now; swing her legs," directed Mabel.

Violet swung the dead woman's legs, Mabel knelt, and they rolled Hilda into the middle of the bed.

"Poor Hilda, this is no way to treat a dead person," lamented Violet.

Mabel flopped beside Hilda, gasping for breath. She heaved herself up and slid off the bed. "We will get her resting properly, then worry about what we did."

Violet and Mabel tugged and turned, straightening Hilda's legs. Rolling her over until she lay flat on her back.

"Okay, let's get the heck out of here."

Violet gently placed Hilda's head on a pillow. "Help me cover her up. It will look more natural when they find her in the morning." She picked the bedspread up off the floor.

"Good idea." Mabel pushed the desk chair out of the way and helped cover the dead woman.

Violet spread one last wrinkle. "Should we maybe take her shoes off?"

"No, it will look more natural; she passed out with her shoes on."

"I guess you're right; this bottle is half empty; she's been drinking crème de menthe," Violet said, indicating the open bottle on the bedside table. "No wonder she was so drunk." She picked up the glass, shaking her head. "I've never liked this stuff; it's too sweet."

Mabel reached for the bottle and sniffed. "Oh, holy crap." She hurriedly set the bottle down.

Violet replaced the glass beside the bottle. "What?"

"That is not crème de menthe. I'd know that smell anywhere; it's antifreeze. I had a radiator leak last fall. That is antifreeze, I'm sure of it."

Violet picked up the glass and sniffed. "Oh my God, you're right. Now what? Someone has murdered Hilda."

"All I can say is thank goodness we have her back in her room. Can you imagine what would have happened if she was found dead in our room? It would be the gulag for us."

"Don't be silly. The Russians don't still have gulags."

"I wouldn't be too sure of that. Regardless, Gulag or jail, I don't want to end up in either." Mabel dashed for the door. Violet grabbed the desk chair. "Wait."

"Wait for what? Let's get out of here."

"Our fingerprints are all over the bottle and glass."

"Oh right, good idea." Mabel, using the hem of her T-shirt, wiped the glass. "Do the bottle," she instructed.

Violet pulled down the sleeve of her sweater and wiped off the bottle.

Mabel looked at the white, waxy face of the dead woman lying on the bed. The life force that was Hilda drained away, her eyes wide open, sunk back into her skull, jaw slackened, and lips pale. "Come on, we have to get the hell out of here."

"Shouldn't we look for clues first?" asked Violet.

"Clues, what clues? We just erased them."

"But don't you want to find out who killed Hilda?"

"We're in a foreign country." Mabel started for the door.

"That never stopped you before."

"This time, we are in big trouble."

"Why? We didn't do anything wrong," insisted Violet.

Mabel paused, grim-faced; she looked back at the dead woman. "Really! We haven't done anything wrong? We moved a dead body and interfered in a crime scene."

# Chapter Twenty-Five

The rain had stopped, and the morning sunlight streamed through the bedroom window. Mabel threw off her bedcovers, looking bleary-eyed over at Violet in her bed. "Did you sleep?" she asked.

"Hardly at all. We have done a terrible injustice to Hilda. Not to mention tampering with a crime scene."

"I know."

Violet sat up in bed. "If the killer left fingerprints, we wiped them off."

"But we had no choice; our fingerprints were on there, too," Mabel said. "Let's get showered. We have to go down to breakfast and act like we don't know Hilda is dead."

"I feel so guilty. I don't know how I'm going to pull this off."

"Violet, you have to, number one. We don't want the authorities to know what we did. If they do, we're sunk." Mabel sat on the edge of her bed. "And number two, the biggest reason we have to act like we know nothing of Hilda's demise is that the killer might give themselves away. We have to be on the lookout for the murderer just in case we get implicated."

# THE SUSPECTS

SHOWERED AND READY for the tour, they closed their door and walked down the hallway, past Hilda's room, on the way to the elevator.

"Look," Violet gasped, grabbing Mabel's arm and pointing to a sign hanging on the dead woman's door. It read, '*Do not disturb.*'

"Oh, my God. Keep on walking," urged Mabel. She pressed the call button for the elevator. "What the heck?"

"I know, this is weird. We did not imagine last night."

Before Violet could reply, Sam and Verity joined them, followed by Allan and Bridget. Good mornings were exchanged as the elevator door opened, and Carmilla and Herman stepped back, making room for them to enter. Leon jogged down the hallway, stepping in just before the doors closed.

"Where were you last night?" asked Carmilla as she made room for Leon.

"Why? What is it to you?" asked Allan. Bridget elbowed her husband and shook her head. Allen shrugged.

"Not you, Allen. Mabel and Violet. We missed you ladies at supper."

"We," Violet searched for a word. "We—"

"We ordered room service," blurted Mabel. "I, we, we were too tired to go down for supper."

"That's an unnecessary expense. The meal was included in the tour package," Herman said.

"And you two were late coming down for supper," remarked Sam, eyeing Allan and Bridget. "We were ready to leave when you two arrived."

"We went for a walk."

"In the rain?" asked Carmilla.

"How romantic," gushed Verity, snuggling up to her husband.

Herman frowned. "Really, it was raining cats and dogs out there."

"We had an umbrella," answered Bridget.

"Anyway, it's none of your business," snapped Allen. Allan and Herman glowered at each other.

Out walking in the rain? They sure made an issue out of standing in it. Allen even tried going into the hotel via the small door. Mabel glanced at Violet. But Violet was staring straight ahead. The elevator stopped on the next floor. Two young people with backpacks jammed in, followed by Sheila and Fred.

Herman crowded against Bridget, who pressed herself away from him, squeezing up beside Leon.

"I'm starved," commented Fred.

"I don't see how. Last night, you ate way more than is good for you," scolded Sheila. "Mind you, supper was fabulous." She craned her neck to look at Herman. "Too bad you and Carmilla missed it. The borscht and beef bourguignon were delicious."

Mabel arched one eyebrow. If Carmilla and Herman weren't in the dining room, how did Carmilla know that she and Violet missed supper? Herman had vowed to get even with Hilda. Was Carmilla creating an alibi for Herman?

"We didn't miss supper; we were just a little late," contradicted Herman.

"Ah, so you were late too. Walking in the rain, were you?" Allan smirked.

Mabel watched Herman glaring back at Allan. Two more to add to her list of suspects.

"Really? I didn't see you two. You must have been very late because Fred and I sat in the dining room for a very long time. We were sitting with the Patels. You know, the couple from India, what friendly people, they were so entertaining. Our next trip is to India," Sheila boasted.

"More souvenirs," muttered Fred.

The elevator stopped on the ground floor, and everyone stepped out.

Mabel tugged Violet's arm as they made their way to the breakfast buffet and whispered in her ear. "Herman and Carmilla and Allan and Bridget. Missing from supper, we can put them on our suspect list."

"Yes, but what about that, do not disturb sign on Hilda's door? Maybe we were wrong. And she was just passed out."

"That, I'm afraid, is wishful thinking. We tugged and pulled on poor old Hilda. Don't you think she would have said something? Seriously, you and I both know dead from passed out."

"I know," Violet whispered. "But the sign?"

"I haven't a clue. Something weird is going on."

"No kidding. So what do we do now?"

"Nothing, we get in line for breakfast. We're stuck with what we did. There is nothing we can do."

After breakfast, they gathered in the lobby, waiting for the tour guides. Mabel's tummy grumbled nervously. She shouldn't have eaten so much breakfast. Her friend fidgeted, shifting from foot to foot. She hoped Violet wouldn't accidentally spill the beans; dear Violet hated subterfuge.

"Dear friends, today we are off first to see the amazing Moscow subway, which will take us to Red Square. There you will see Lenin's tomb. And visit Saint Basil's Cathedral. We won't be going by bus. So, I hope you have your walking shoes on. Today, I will be your tour director. Hilda is indisposed."

"Hungover most like," snickered Bert to his wife, Cindy.

Mabel exchanged a puzzled look with Violet as they followed Annika out the hotel doors onto the street. Did Annika put out the do not disturb sign? And if she did? Why? Had she killed Hilda and was buying more time? Mabel could not get the thoughts of Annika as the killer of Hilda from her mind. She would keep an eye on her and see if the woman gave any sign that she knew Hilda was dead. But what sign would that be?

They rode the crowded escalator from the street-side to the subway below. The steep incline made Mabel's tummy wobble; she leaned backward, afraid she would fall. The descent took three long minutes. She heaved a shaky sigh of relief when they reached the bottom.

"Dear friends, gather around me. We will not be taking the subway directly to Red Square. I want you to see all the amazing stations. So, follow me, and please be quick to get off the subway. Be as quick as you can. If you don't get off, we will lose you. But if we do, do not be afraid. You can continue to Red Square, and we will meet up there." She handed each member a schedule for the subway.

The first station platform amazed Mabel. It had a yellow dome ceiling decorated with frescoes, marble columns, and massive ornate chandeliers. They barely had time to take it in before Annika herded them back onto the subway. Each station they stopped at was incredible and different. Some had white dome ceilings with stained glass decorations. Others were decorated with mosaic tiles. Some of the stations had paintings depicting rural life. One station had a statue of three revolutionary men holding guns and a flag. All were brightly lit with enormous chandeliers, marble columns, and tiled floors. The subway stations resembled an art museum.

Annika ushered them up another steep escalator to street level, and they paraded into Red Square. The air, fresh from the previous day's rain, was welcoming after the subway's stale smells and noise.

"It is really red," commented Verity, hanging on to her husband's arm.

Annika took a headcount. "We have lost Allan and Bridget. But they are world travellers. I am sure they will either turn up here or at the hotel. In case they return to the hotel, I will alert Hilda."

Mabel's eyes narrowed as she watched Annika put her cell phone to her ear. Was she establishing an alibi by pretending not to know Hilda was dead? Mabel then turned her gaze to her fellow tour members. Watching for any signs of guilty nervousness. But there was none she could detect. Most were already taking pictures of Red Square.

Verity, wearing walking shoes instead of high heels, hung onto Sam's arm, chatting excitedly with her husband. Mabel lifted her eyebrows; for once, the girl seemed to be flirting with her own husband. Sheila, checking a list of some sort, mumbled about Russian stacking dolls. Fred, looking over her shoulder at the list, sighed. Herman was strutting around like he didn't have a care in the world. He wasn't at the supper last evening, and he despised Hilda. But enough to kill her? Mabel dismissed Carmilla as a suspect out of hand, but then it was Carmilla who gave the impression they were at supper. And Sheila and Fred never saw them there. And Leon, had he been at the supper last night? Mabel looked around. Where was Leon? He was with them when they left the subway. But now he, too, was missing.

Annika sighed and pocketed her phone. "I'll try again later. Perhaps they are here already, exploring. Now let me tell you about Moscow's famous Red Square. Krasni is red in Russian; it can mean beautiful or excellent. But as you can see, the Kremlin and the fortress wall are made from red brick."

"It looks so familiar. I guess because I've seen it on so many newscasts," Violet marvelled.

"The Red Square is eight hundred thousand square feet. This long, beautiful building on the east side of this square is, of course, the Kremlin. And Lenin's Tomb is over there." Indicated Annika.

Mabel listened as the young tour director rattled off facts about Red Square. If Annika did kill Hilda, she was certainly a cool customer.

"As you can see, at the square's southern end is Saint Basil's Cathedral." Annika led them across the square toward the cathedral. Its brilliant onion domes of green, blue, red, and white gleamed in the sunlight, each dome a different design.

"This magnificent cathedral was built by Ivan the Terrible. Legend says that he had the Italian architect blinded. So he couldn't replicate the design. Stalin wanted the church demolished, but the Soviet architect, Baranovsky, prevented it. And was sent to the Gulag for his troubles." Annika turned, indicating a long, three-level red building with a glass roof. "This is a department store called GUM. Sheila, you will be happy to know that in this department store, you will find Louis Vuitton and Prada, as well as many gourmet food outlets with wine and chocolate."

"Oh, can we stop?" Sheila asked excitedly.

"Not now, I'm afraid. Next is the Armoury."

"Great, I'm looking forward to seeing the armour. And the weapons from ages past," Herman said.

"I'm not going," announced Sheila. "I don't want to see a bunch of old weapons and armour. I'm going shopping at the Gum. Come on, Fred."

"Yes, dear," mumbled Fred.

"The name Armoury is deceiving," interjected Annika. "It is one of the oldest museums in Russia. At one time, it was used to store weapons and household items for the Tsars. But today, you will see the ivory throne of Ivan the Terrible. The imperial carriages and sleds that were used by Catherine the Great. Gowns, jewelry and the famous Fabergé eggs. And much more."

"Oh, then I will come. Is there a souvenir shop?" asked Sheila.

Watching from across the square, a short, squat man with a bushy black beard and a yellow and red scarf.

---

MABEL, BONE-TIRED, trudged behind the tour group through the body scanner into the hotel lobby. It was an effort to put one foot in front of the other. With very little sleep, she'd toured the Moscow sights. And always at the back of her mind lurked the fact someone killed Hilda. And the puzzling 'Do not disturb' sign on the dead woman's hotel room door. As she crossed the lobby, she spotted Allan and Bridget sitting in the lounge.

"There you are," greeted Annika. "We lost you on the subway. I am sorry you missed Saint Basil's and Red Square."

"We enjoyed our day; we got to see all the platforms, which were amazing, just like you said."

"A pity you didn't get to see the Red Square," Leon said. "It was remarkable, just like what you see on the news."

Mabel's eyes narrowed. Leon, where had the man popped up from? Leon had not been on the Red Square tour. Why was he lying?

"Bridget and I plan on going out later on our own to explore. We have the subway schedule."

"Please be back for our dinner and the theatre," Annika cautioned; she turned to face the group. "Those of you who chose the ballet can eat later. But those that have chosen the Cossack performance should eat at the early sitting. In case you have forgotten which one you picked, I will post the list on the bulletin board by the elevator. Please read the lists so there is no confusion." She rifled through her black leather case. "I do not seem to have the lists. Please wait while I call Hilda." She took her phone from her pocket and punched a number. Annika tapped her toe on the carpet as she waited. The tour group milled around the lounge, chatting and showing each other pictures they took of the tour on their cell phones and cameras. Mabel watched Annika's frustration grow. Annika's toe now thumped a rapid tattoo as she waited for Hilda to answer.

Pocketing her phone, she said. "I know most of you are anxious to go to your rooms, but please wait here. I won't be long, I promise. And Allen and Bridget, please don't go sightseeing just yet. Please wait here in the lobby. It is important we get the schedule for the ballet and the Cossack performance. I'll just pop up and talk to Hilda. It won't take long."

Mabel's tiredness disappeared. Now was the time to clear up the do not disturb sign and maybe discover who the killer was. She poked Violet with her elbow. Violet, showing Mrs. Patel her pictures on her camera, frowned. Mabel did a head tilt toward Annika. Violet's eyes darted from Mabel to Annika. She excused herself, turned off her camera, and followed Mabel, joining Annika at the elevator.

"I think it would be best if you waited with the others," Annika said.

"We will be just a few minutes. I need to freshen up. And Violet has our itinerary. I think we picked the Cossack dancing."

Annika gave them a worried look. "Okay, fine. If you have the schedule. But please do not be late for supper; it's the early sitting."

"We won't be late, I promise you," Mabel said. The elevator doors closed, and Annika pressed the button for their floor. While Violet looked with pity at the young tour director, Mabel's eyes held suspicion. "When did Hilda tell you she wasn't conducting the tour this morning?" she asked.

"Hilda texted me last night."

"What time was that?"

Annika flashed Mabel an irritated look. "Why?"

"No reason, I just wondered, is all." Was Annika lying? She wanted to see Annika's reaction when she discovered Hilda's dead body. She was sure she would be able to tell if Annika was faking a shocked surprise. The doors opened, and they followed Annika off the elevator and down the corridor.

Annika stopped at Hilda's room. The 'Do not disturb' sign still hung on the doorknob. Mabel and Violet stood by her side.

Annika gave them a sidelong look. "I thought you were going to freshen up?"

"Right, come on, Mabel." Violet tugged on her arm. Reluctantly, Mabel followed her to their room, and Violet slid the keycard into the card reader.

"Darn, I have my suspicions about that woman. If Annika has a keycard, we'll know for sure she is lying. Maybe she went back after poisoning Hilda to make sure she was dead. And put out that do not disturb sign to buy her an alibi."

"Hush." Violet opened their bedroom door a crack and peered out. "Be quiet, and I'll tell you what I can see."

Mabel bit her lip, shifting from foot to foot in anticipation.

"Annika is rapping on the door, so she doesn't have a keycard. Now she has her phone out. She's talking on her phone." Violet swivelled back to face Mabel. "She can't be talking to Hilda. Good Lord, were we wrong?"

"More wishful thinking. Just keep a lookout."

"Yes, you're right. But I so wish we were wrong," Violet said. "Annika is pacing back and forth in front of Hilda's door. She is still talking on her phone. Oh, she has pocketed her phone. Now she appears to be waiting."

"We should join her and ask what the heck is going on. I want to be there when she opens the door. That texting story may be just that, a story, and all those phone calls to Hilda could be her creating more of an alibi. I want to see her reaction when she steps into the room."

"Okay, let's go. No, wait, I need a sheet of paper."

Mabel gave Violet a puzzled look. "A sheet of paper?"

"You said I had the schedule. It will look like I have."

Mabel shrugged. "Well, you don't."

"It doesn't matter. Any old paper will do."

"Any old paper, that's silly," Mabel said.

"The sheet of paper will be so she won't suspect we used the schedule as a ruse," explained Violet.

"Seriously, you think after she finds a dead body, she is going to notice if we have a schedule or not?"

"I guess not." Violet opened the door a little wider. "Alright, let's join Annika. A maid is coming down the corridor. She probably has the master key."

"Go, go." They sprinted out the door, then changed their pace to walk sedately down the corridor.

The maid and Annika were conversing in Russian. The maid took a keycard from her pocket. Mabel, followed closely by Violet, sped up and hurried to the door just as the maid opened it. The maid stood back as Annika entered the room and switched on the lights. Mabel pushed her way past the maid, following Annika into the room.

Hilda's white, waxy corpse lay on the bed, a knife in her chest.

# Chapter Twenty-Six

"Oh my God," gasped Mabel, putting a hand to her mouth.

"Aaaah, oh, no, no, no," screamed Annika. The colour drained from her face, and she stumbled back from the bed. Mabel grabbed her and guided her to the desk chair.

Violet gulped, her eyes widened. "Hilda has been stabbed."

"I, I must do something," white and shaking Annika mumbled weakly.

Mabel turned to the maid, who was standing in the doorway. The woman's mouth hung open, and her face was ashen. "Do you speak English?" Mabel asked her.

"Da," gasped the maid, shrinking back toward the corridor. Mabel looked blank.

"Da, yes." The maid trembled, nodding her head. "This woman, this woman. She is killed?"

"Yes, killed; call the front desk and request the police to come."

"The police," shrieked the maid, backing suddenly out of the room.

Mabel hurried to the door, following her out into the corridor. "Yes, the police. Tell the manager or whoever is at the desk to call the police."

"No, nyet, nyet."

"Da, I'm afraid so. The police must be called."

"Da, da, afraid."

"No, I am not afraid. We must call for the police," urged Mabel.

The maid, her lips quivering, backed up further into the hallway, shaking her head. "Nyet," she cried, turned, and fled down the corridor and around a corner.

Mabel hurriedly returned to the room, raising her hands in a helpless shrug. "Now what?"

"I'll do it. The people at the front desk will speak English. You look after Annika." Violet picked up the phone to dial.

"Your fingerprints," Mabel whispered.

"We wiped them," Violet murmured and pressed the button on the phone for the desk.

"Your fingerprints will be on the phone," Mabel hissed.

"Get a grip," Violet hissed back. "My prints don't matter now. I have to use the phone." She put up a hand, halting a reply from Mabel. "Front desk? Yes, everything is fine. No, I mean everything is not fine. We need the police." Violet grimaced and waited. "Yes, da, someone is hurt. Well, more than hurt." Violet paused and shook her head. "No, a doctor won't help. We need the police." After another long pause, Violet sighed and said, "Well, then send a doctor if you must. But for goodness' sake, send the police." She ended the phone conversation with the room number.

Annika rose from the chair, cautiously going to the bedside. Her hand reached out tentatively to touch the lifeless figure lying dead in the bed with a knife sticking in her chest. Hilda's dead eyes stared back at her. Annika quickly withdrew her hand and sagged. "That knife, oh my God, a knife." She broke into loud sobs.

"Sit down, dear; Violet has phoned the front desk. They are sending for the police."

Annika, weeping, sank back onto the desk chair. Her shoulders shook. Tears streamed down her cheeks. "Should I do something? Poor Hilda, I don't know what to do?"

"There, there, dear, there is no need for you to do anything. The police will be here shortly. Would you like some water?" Violet opened the water bottle and picked up the glass on the bedside table.

"No. Not that glass," shrieked Mabel.

Violet held the bottle, ready to pour. "This might settle her down a bit; it can't hurt."

"Yes, it can; the glass is dirty," Mabel said each word slowly.

Violet eyed the glass.

"Germs. Hilda might have drunk from this glass."

"Oh, my gosh," uttered Violet, slamming the bottle and glass down on the bedside table.

Annika looked at the dead body lying on the bed. She put her hands over her eyes. "She looks so grotesque, that terrible knife," she said, her wails becoming louder.

"I know, dear, death isn't pretty. Maybe it's best if you stop looking at Hilda," Mabel said, turning the desk chair so Annika was no longer facing the bed.

Violet vigorously wiped the glass and water bottle. "Oh my God, I forgot," Violet yelped.

"Then, for goodness' sake, wipe your prints now," whispered Mabel, rushing to the bedside table.

"I did."

"The phone receiver? I told you to wipe it," Mabel, speaking in a harsh undertone, picked up the phone and rubbed the receiver with her sleeve.

"Leave the darn phone alone," hissed Violet. "They'll know I used it. I phoned the desk." Violet took the receiver from Mabel and placed it on the cradle. Tugging on Mabel's sleeve, she asked, "So, what are we going to do?"

"Wait for the police. There is nothing more we can do. But I should check to see if that maid came back. I wonder why she is so afraid?"

"It's Russia."

"Oh, right."

"But the knife, why the knife? Why did they stab Hilda?" hissed Violet.

"I know, I know. It's crazy." Mabel shook her head. "It doesn't make sense. But we can talk about it later." She tilted her head at Annika, who was silently crying.

Violet looked at the dead body and then at Annika. She grabbed Mabel's arm. "Annika is in the desk chair," she said softly.

"Yes, Annika looked like she was ready to faint. I don't think she killed Hilda," Mabel said in a hushed voice. "In fact, I'm sure of it. The poor girl is a mess."

Violet rolled her eyes and sighed loudly; she bent and whispered into Mabel's ear. "There are two."

"Two what?"

"Two desk chairs," blurted Violet.

# Chapter Twenty-Seven

There was a light tap on the door. Mabel opened the door to find three men. Two men were in uniform, and the third in civilian attire.

Clicking the heels of his black oxford shoes together, the slim, smartly dressed man announced, "I am the hotel manager, Dimitri Kuznetsov." He smiled at the two women standing side by side in the doorway. "You have a problem? How may we be of service?" The two uniformed police officers stood on either side of the manager; one officer, a small, roly-poly middle-aged man, reminded Mabel of a cherub without wings. The taller of the two men was a young, slim, blond-haired man. His rigid stance looked military.

Annika rose as the three men entered, wiping the tears from her cheeks with the palms of her hands. Taking a deep breath, she adjusted her jacket with the tour logo and addressed them in Russian.

Mabel and Violet stepped back, revealing the dead body. Dimitri Kuznetsov cautiously approached the bed. He let out a shocked cry, his hand over his mouth. He turned to look at the two women who crowded up beside him, then at Annika. Annika, averting her eyes, wrung her hands.

The police officers brushed the manager aside; they stood looking at the dead body with the knife in her chest; they then exchanged a rapid-fire conversation in Russian.

"This is why you called for these officers and me?" asked Dimitri, the hotel manager; his eyes darted from the body on the bed to Violet and Mabel.

Mabel rolled her eyes and opened her mouth. Before she could speak, Violet shot her a piercing look. Mabel raised her shoulders and clamped her lips shut.

"I'm the one who called you," Violet volunteered.

"You found this woman like, like this?" stuttered the manager, his professional demeanour giving way to shock and confusion.

"Yes," Violet replied. "My friend Mabel and I, and of course Annika Nilsson our,... our tour director.

"We found poor Hilda just as you see," Mabel said.

The hotel manager turned to the officers, speaking to them in Russian. Mabel and Violet's heads swivelled back and forth as if watching a tennis match as the officers and the manager conversed. A knock on the door interrupted the conversation. The tall blond officer opened the door.

A portly man in an ill-fitting black suit carrying a brown leather satchel burst into the room. The manager rushed over and shook the man's hand. "Dakter," he said, ushering him to the bedside.

Mabel and Violet looked questioningly at Annika. "This gentleman is the doctor," she explained.

The doctor, muttering under his breath, paused, looking at the dead woman on the bed, then back at the hotel manager.

# THE SUSPECTS

He uttered a few guttural words in Russian, pointed at the knife, and threw up his hands, shaking his head.

Annika wiped her nose with the back of her hand, sighed, looked sadly at Mabel and Violet and said, "The doctor says there is nothing he can do; Hilda is dead."

"Big surprise there," Mabel muttered under her breath.

The doctor spoke a few more terse words in Russian, nodded to the manager, shook hands with the two bewildered-looking police officers, and quickly left the room.

Violet reached into her pocket and offered Annika a tissue. Annika, accepting the tissue, wiped her nose. "I will ask the officers if you may leave. This is so distressing for you." Keeping her eyes down, clutching the tissue tightly in her fist, she took a deep breath and made her request in Russian.

There were shrugs and more muttering between the police officers. Finally, the cherub officer turned to address Annika.

Annika looked with a tear-stained face at Mabel and Violet. "I am sorry, the officers are unsure how to proceed. They think they should wait for their superiors before permitting you to leave the room."

"Why? Do they think we had something to do with this?" asked Mabel. She wished they never followed Annika. Her curiosity could be her downfall.

"I will ask."

"No, no, don't ask," Mabel said hurriedly, afraid of the answer.

"Couldn't we just go to our room? Then we would be out of everyone's way," suggested Violet.

The manager glanced at the women and then spoke rapidly to the officers. Annika, speaking in Russian, interrupted the man. She sniffed and wiped her nose with the tissue, gesturing to Mabel and Violet, and the hotel manager nodded.

Annika turned to Mabel and Violet. "I told them you were very upset and needed to lie down."

Mabel thought that was rich; it was Annika who had nearly collapsed, but whatever worked as long as they could leave.

The two officers whispered, glancing at the women. Finally, the cherub officer nodded and turned to speak in hushed tones to the manager.

Dimitri Kuznetsov gave Annika a sad smile and relayed the information in English. "These two ladies are permitted to return to their accommodations accompanied by Officer Smirnov." He indicated the roly-poly cherub officer. "Annika Nilsson, you will stay here with Officer Yahontov and me."

Annika's jaw dropped; she looked appalled. "Oh, no, I must leave. I can not stay here." Her voice cracked. She swallowed and continued. "I must go. I have people from the tour waiting for me."

After another rapid-fire exchange in Russian, Annika sighed and slumped back in the desk chair, shredding the tissue in her lap.

"Oh no, do you have to stay?" asked Mabel.

"Never mind, I will be fine. I guess...I guess it is only proper someone who knew Hilda...should," her voice broke. "I should stay with her."

With one last look at a forlorn Annika, Mabel reluctantly followed Violet and Officer Smirnov out the door.

# Chapter Twenty-Eight

The short, cherubic man gave the two women a friendly smile as they walked along the hallway. Mabel smiled back; she hoped the man stayed outside their room so she and Violet could talk freely. Maybe the officer didn't understand English, or maybe he did. After all, this was Russia; she'd seen spy movies.

To Mabel's relief, Officer Smirnov planted himself outside their door. "Good Lord, do you believe what has happened." She sank down on the edge of her bed.

"I feel so guilty for letting poor Annika discover Hilda. And I feel bad we left her. The poor girl is barely holding herself together."

"I know, even though Hilda was such a witch to her, Annika is having a hard time with her death. But we had no choice. If the Russian police say go, I'm pretty sure you have to do what they say."

"She's probably never seen a dead body before."

"Well, for sure, never one with a knife sticking into her."

"This is so weird. A twice murdered woman," Violet said, sinking onto the bed beside Mabel.

"Wait." Mabel jumped up from the bed and raced to the bathroom.

"Are you okay? Are you sick?"

"Come in here."

Violet rushed to the bathroom. The shower was turned on full blast, and Mabel was sitting on the edge of the tub. "Sit here," she said, indicating the toilet and closing the lid.

"What? Why?"

"Sit down and listen," directed Mabel.

"In here?"

"Yes, in here. Our room might be bugged. They could be listening to everything we say."

"They?"

"Yes, they. We are in Russia. Our room could be bugged. That's why I'm running the water, to cover our conversation."

"I'm not staying in this steamy little room. This is silly. Get a grip."

"What do you mean, a grip?"

"A grip on reality." Violet stomped out of the bathroom.

"They could be listening," muttered Mabel. She shut off the shower and came out of the bathroom to dry her hands.

"Why would they be listening?" Violet made quotation marks in the air with her fingers. "Who would be interested in tourists?"

"We might be spies," Mabel said, tossing the towel onto the luggage rack.

"You watch too many spy movies. If they are listening now, they were listening last night. And they, whoever they are, will know we moved Hilda."

"Yes, I guess," Mabel agreed reluctantly. Tugging on her damp T-shirt, she yanked it off. "Where were we?"

"Can we leave your delusions and get back to the murder?"

"My delusions? Hump." Mabel rummaged in her suitcase.

"You have a very suspicious nature."

"And you are way too trusting." Mabel pulled a bright red T-shirt over her head.

"Maybe," agreed Violet. "Anyway, back to the murder. Why would someone poison Hilda and then stab her?"

"And how did they get into her room? And was it the same killer? Why? It's a little like Rasputin." Mabel gave a hollow laugh.

"For someone who said they didn't care who murdered Hilda. You are sure showing a lot of interest."

"Did I say I wasn't interested?"

"Yes, you did."

"Okay, Maybe I did. But that was before I realized we left evidence behind in that room. We could be charged with accessory to the murder." Mabel began to pace.

"You mean the chair?"

Mabel stopped her pacing and turned to Violet. "Yes, they are bound to think it's odd that Hilda's room has two desk chairs. And if they check our room, they will find none. Think about it. How do you think the Russian police will react if they find out we moved Hilda's body and wiped fingerprints?"

"I don't want to think about it."

"Why, oh why, didn't we remember to take the darn chair?" Mabel continued to pace.

"We should have just left poor Hilda in our desk chair and taken hers."

"I know. But it's too late to think about that now. Hilda's room has two, and ours has none." Mabel stopped pacing and said, "Maybe we could steal a chair from someone else's room?"

Violet threw up her hands and asked, "How?"

"I don't know. Maybe we could wait until a maid is cleaning a room. I'll distract her, and you steal the chair."

"Me? Steal the chair?" Violet shook her head.

"Okay, you distract the maid, and I'll steal the chair."

"I doubt we could do it. And besides, if we did, we'd be framing some innocent soul for murder."

"I'm not sure we would be framing anyone for murder?"

Violet crossed her arms and gave Mabel a stern look. "I don't care. I'm not stealing a chair. Besides, our fingerprints would still be on that chair in Hilda's room."

"Okay, okay. I guess you're right. We won't steal a chair. And maybe we shouldn't even worry about the chair? It's not the murder weapon, but on the other hand, it is a link. As you pointed out. Our fingerprints are all over it."

"You think they will fingerprint us?" Violet asked.

"Of course they will. If I were the police, I'd line the lot of us up and fingerprint every tour member. There's a knife sticking into Hilda's chest. And we are the people who knew her. It's not like some random person stumbled into her room and poisoned her and then stuck a knife in her for good measure."

"Our fingerprints aren't on the knife."

"True, but our prints are all over that darn chair. Like I said before, we could be charged with accessory to the murder. We need to find out who killed Hilda and why?"

"Obviously, it was someone she knew," Violet said, "It's not a random killing. The killer is someone from our tour group. Herman despised her. Who else?"

"The Hughes. Allan and Bridget are a suspicious pair. And so is Leon Peeters; he's always popping up and disappearing. He lied today, saying he was at Red Square. And don't forget the scarf men. We've seen men wearing those red and yellow scarves, but I don't see the connection. No, it has to be someone on the bus tour." Mabel slumped on the bed beside Violet.

"Maybe it isn't the same person. Maybe we have two people who wanted her dead. Two killers."

"Well, technically, one. Hilda was already dead when she was stabbed."

"Right, but how did they get into her room? Mabel, do you still have the keycard to Hilda's room?"

"I think so."

"You think?"

"What was I wearing? Oh yeah, those darn tight jeans and that gold mermaid shirt I bought in Copenhagen. I never got a chance to change clothes before Hilda ended up dead in our room." Mabel jumped up, rummaging through her dirty laundry. She yanked out her jeans, digging through the pockets. "It's not here. Oh, Lord. I must have left the card."

"Great, the extra desk chair with our fingerprints and now the keycard."

"With my fingerprints on it."

# Chapter Twenty-Nine

A sharp rap on their hotel room door caused Mabel to cast a worried look at Violet; she hurried to open the door. Officer Smirnov stood in the doorway. He said something in Russian; it sounded to Mabel like a command. She nervously shrugged. And spread her hands in a gesture of I have no idea what you said. Did the police know they'd moved Hilda's body? Did someone see them? "Do you think we are being arrested?" murmured Mabel apprehensively to Violet. She took in a deep breath, willing herself to remain calm, but her stomach churned. This wasn't Canada. What next?

Violet, clasping Mabel's icy hand in hers, smiled hopefully at the Russian police officer.

The little man smiled back, bobbing his head up and down in a friendly way, beckoning them to follow. They passed Hilda's hotel room; the door was shut, and an officer they hadn't seen before stood guard outside. Officer Yahontov, waiting for them at the elevator, gave them a forbidding look. As they rode down to the main floor, Mabel looked from officer to officer. Smirnov seemed the friendliest of the two as he smiled; the other police officer, grim-faced, looked down at her. Mabel gulped and squeezed Violet's hand.

# THE SUSPECTS

As they emerged from the elevator, they met six uniformed police officers ready to board. One, wearing a paper facemask, had an array of cameras slung over his shoulder. The others were carrying black leather bags; all were wearing latex gloves. The officers escorting Mabel and Violet paused to exchange a few words.

A white-faced Annika stood by the door to the lounge; the girl squared her shoulders and pushed open the door. Yahonotov and Smirnov hustled Mabel and Violet into the lounge behind her. The officers then took up positions on either side of the door. A young couple and a small boy attempted to enter. Officer Yahontov barked out a sharp demand in Russian. The couple and their son turned and hurried away. At the back of the room, a waiter was serving drinks to some of the tour members. Smirnov issued a guttural command, and the waiter quickly set the drink tray down on a long table at the back of the room and sped out, closing the door behind him. Drinks in hand, the group at the back of the room turned to face the officers, bewildered looks on their faces.

Mr. and Mrs. Patel sat on a backless leather couch under long white lace-curtained windows, chatting and sharing colourful brochures with two young Japanese women. The sharp command stopped Mr. Patel in mid-sentence. He looked at the police officers and nudged his wife. Mrs. Patel's eyes widened, and her lips formed a silent oh.

Bert and Cindy, lounging on a small olive-green loveseat, exchanged puzzled looks. "What's up? Do we need guards? Is there a threat of some kind?" Bert asked, setting his empty drink glass on a glass-topped coffee table. Allan and Bridget sat on another olive-green loveseat with a city map spread out on their knees. Their eyes darted to the police officers at the door. Hurriedly, Allan folded the map and stuck it into one of the pockets on his vest.

Opposite Allan and Bridget sat Herman and Carmilla. "Annika, what the hell is the hold-up? Can't we please learn the schedule?" Herman asked. "We've been waiting forever. We all have better things to do."

Closing a glossy magazine on her lap, Carmilla admonished her husband, "Shush dear, I think something has happened. Annika looks like she has been crying."

Leaning up against the wall with his phone to his ear, Leon eyed the officers by the door. The door swung open, and Bjorn strode in; he gave the group a big grin and took up a position beside Leon. Leon tucked his phone into his pocket and shook hands with Bjorn.

Verity glanced up from her perch on the arm of a wingback chair. Stroking her husband's sparse hair, she smiled over the top of his head at Bjorn.

With an annoyed look at his wife, Sam grasped her hand and stopped the caress. Verity pouted.

"May we sit with you?" Mabel asked Fred and Sheila.

Sheila glanced up from her notepad. "Sure, I'm just checking things off my list. Unfortunately, I still haven't purchased Russian stacking dolls. And I have to agree with Herman; we have been waiting here forever."

Making room for Violet and Mabel, Fred shifted over on the couch. "Damn it, Sheila, don't you have enough stuff?"

Sheila pursed her lips and closed her notepad, jamming the pad into her purse.

Mabel and Violet squeezed onto the couch. Mabel waited; when would someone announce Hilda's demise? And who among her fellow travellers was the cold-blooded killer?

The doors swung open again, and a tall, thin man dressed in a dark suit and tie entered. The black-haired man had a long face with a prominent chin. Taking a military stance, he scanned the room with steely blue eyes.

Annika offered a weak smile, took a deep breath, cleared her throat, and began. "As some of you already know, our dear tour director, Hilda, has met with an unfortunate." Annika paused as if searching for words. "Hilda has met with an accident. And she is... She has died." Annika sank onto a desk chair by the writing desk. "I can not. I am sorry I, I can't..." her voice trailed off.

The tour members gasped, cries of what? Really? Hilda? Filled the room.

Violet looked at Mabel in surprise. "An accident?"

Mabel placed her index finger to her lips, watching the room erupt into many languages as couples chattered loudly among themselves.

Leon pulled his phone out of his pocket, his fingers dancing on the small keypad. Bjorn strode promptly over to Annika and knelt, putting a comforting arm around her. Her shoulders shook as she sobbed.

"Oh no, poor Hilda, so young," lamented Sheila. Then added. "Can we go now? I have to purchase a set of Russian dolls."

"I'm sorry for your loss, Annika," Herman said. "But I hope this doesn't mean we won't get to see the Cossack dancing."

"And the ballet, are we going to the ballet? I so want to see that. Don't you, dear?" Verity kissed her husband's forehead.

"Hilda is dead, and you want entertainment?" snapped Sam. "Besides, you don't know ballet from folk dancing."

Verity looked down at her hands and bit her lip.

"I knew she didn't look good. The woman drank way too much. Probably her liver gave out," Herman said.

"Herman, shut the hell up. You don't know squat. If Hilda died of liver failure, it wouldn't be called an accident," snapped Sam. A shouting match between Sam and Herman broke out.

"Attention, attention," bellowed the black-suited man. His English had a slight Russian accent. The kerfuffle continued unabated. The tall man, muttering in Russian, marched to the writing desk; he picked up a vase, slamming it down on the desk with a thud. The vase shattered, shards flying everywhere. Annika jumped, scrambling away from the desk. Sam and Herman fell silent. The man looked briefly down at the mess, then he continued. "Be quiet. You all must pay attention. I am Inspector Lebedev, and this is a police investigation. I will be conducting this investigation into the death of Miss. Hilda." Lebedev paused and looked over at Officer Yahontov and beckoned. The officer hurried over with a sheet of papers in his hand. Lebedev shuffled the papers, glanced at the notes, and then at the tour group as they began chatting. "Quiet," he commanded. He waited until all were silent, then continued. "We are investigating the suspicious death of Miss Hilda Karlson, a citizen of Denmark."

A collective gasp erupted from the tour group. Bjorn kept a comforting arm around Annika as she pressed a tissue to her nose. Carmilla grasped Herman's arm; Herman shook off her hand. Leon turned to face the window, talking on his phone. Allan glanced at the officers, then at Bridget; she returned his gaze, putting her index finger to her lips. Verity let out a moan and slid off the arm of the chair down onto her husband's lap, burying her head on his shoulder.

"Oh, for God's sake, Verity, stop it. You didn't even like the woman. A few minutes ago, you wanted to watch dancing." Sam stood, dumping her into the chair. Verity, covering her face with her hands, sobbed softly.

"No one liked Hilda. She was a vicious, overbearing harridan. I don't care what Mister Know-it-all thinks." Herman cast a scornful look at Sam. "I think she probably drank herself to death."

Sam scowled at Herman. "What part of suspicious death don't you get?"

"And we must not speak ill of the dead," Carman rebuked.

"Hilda was a nasty piece of work. Everyone here can attest to that," agreed Bert.

Sheila glanced at Mabel, then whispered into her husband's ear.

The excited murmurs amongst the tour group became louder. "Silence," roared the inspector.

The tour members exchanged mutinous glances but obeyed.

"Anyway, what makes you think her death is suspicious?" Herman asked Inspector Lebedev.

"Shush." Carmilla tugged on her husband's sleeve.

"I will ask the questions, you will answer them, and you will remain quiet until I speak to you. Is that clear?"

Herman nodded obediently.

"I see I have a great many suspects," Lebedev said as he surveyed the room with a slight smile on his lips. Abruptly, he turned and addressed Annika. "I want the list containing all the members of your tour group." He then issued a terse command in Russian to Officer Yahontov. The officer nodded, brought his heels together with a click, and sped out the door. Inspector Lebedeve then turned back to Annika, "My officer is arranging for a room for the interrogations."

A lump rose in Mabel's throat, and a chill ran down her spine. Interrogations, they were going to be interrogated!

Mabel wasn't the only one who looked worried. At the mention of interrogations, the murmurs became an uproar of protests. Finally, Smirnov stepped forward, the cherub-faced man's hand resting on the pistol strapped to his belt. "Silence," he yelled in a thick Russian accent.

The tour members looked at the cherub man in surprise. Mabel gulped, and Violet grasped her hand.

"Attention, silence, silence," Lebedev shouted. The group's complaints became murmurs. And Smirnov stepped back to the door.

Annika wiped her cheeks with her hands, took a deep breath, and said, "Please, my group is missing out on their last night in Moscow. There is still time for some of my group to take in the ballet performance."

Lebedev replied sharply, his lips curled. "There will be no touring; you and your tour group are confined to this hotel. I am sorry your tourists will not see our famous ballet. But a woman has been murdered."

The tour group gasped.

"Do you not want the murderer to pay for the crime? Did you not like your boss?" He looked with cold suspicion at the young tour director. "Perhaps you would like us to question you again. Perhaps we did not find our answers when we first interviewed you."

"I...I have nothing to hide. I have nothing to add to my statement. And, of course, I want the killer of dear Hilda to be found. The ballet is of no importance," stumbling over her reply, Annika sank onto a couch.

"Good. I will conduct the interviews." The imposing officer scanned the room with his cold, steely eyes. "And I will get a confession."

# Chapter Thirty

One by one, Officer Smirnov took the tour members away to be questioned. The remaining members stood in small groups. Speaking softly and giving Yahontov, who remained by the door, wary looks. Those who returned looked a little less anxious. Most were quite talkative and excited by their interviews, exclaiming they couldn't wait to tell their friends back home how they were part of a murder investigation in Russia. Others headed straight for the buffet the hotel staff set up in the lounge.

Mabel, sitting on a window seat, waited nervously for her turn. Maybe someone witnessed them trundling Hilda back to her room. And where was Leon? He'd volunteered to be the first member of their group to be interviewed. She poked Violet in the ribs and whispered, "Leon isn't back from his interview with the police. I knew there was something fishy about that man."

"But if he is guilty, why are the police still questioning us?" Violet whispered back. She tugged the printed scarf off her neck, rapidly folding it into squares.

"I don't know. I actually hope we are next. I'm getting more nervous by the minute. I just want this over with."

"Maybe someone will confess first," Violet replied in a hushed tone, unfolding her scarf and twisting one end into a tiny point.

"That darn keycard. I'm worried about it. Do you think the police have fingerprinted anyone?" murmured Mabel, chewing on a thumbnail. "No one has said anything?"

"Let's hope they aren't. I guess we'll find out soon enough when it's our turn." Violet's eyes danced around at her companions as she pressed the wrinkles in her scarf out, then began to pleat it.

"Yeah, right," Mabel replied. Her stomach was in knots, and she wiped her sweaty palms on her slacks. She looked at Officer Yahontov, stationed by the exit, munching on a bun filled with meat dripping a creamy filling that he licked off his fingers.

"Maybe we should eat now. Sheila is with the police. She is probably quizzing the inspector about the best place to buy Russian dolls," Violet nervously joked as she twisted her scarf into a ball.

Mabel tried to laugh, but it died on her lips. "I couldn't eat a thing, maybe after the interview."

"It will be fine," reassured Violet. "We've done nothing wrong." She unrolled her scarf. Her hand shook as she pressed out the wrinkles.

"Nothing wrong besides moving a dead body and interfering with the crime scene, and our fingerprints are all over the place." The word Gulag danced in Mabel's brain.

"Not all over the place. Don't exaggerate. And remember, it would be a lot worse if she were found murdered in our room.

Mind you, there would be no knife," Violet whispered back, folding her scarf into smaller and smaller squares.

The door opened, and Sheila entered, appearing excited by her experience. She rushed up to Mabel and exclaimed in hushed tones, "I'm sorry, Mabel, but I had to tell the inspector about you and dear Hilda."

Mabel's jaw dropped.

Violet gasped. "What did you say?"

"I had to tell the truth," Sheila said; she hurried away, leaving a perplexed Mabel and Violet.

Uttering a sharp command in Russian, Officer Smirnov pointed to Mabel, motioning her to follow. Mabel rose, her heart pounded, and her stomach churned.

Violet stood, straightened her shoulders, and stuck out her chin. She screwed her scarf up into a ball, jamming it into her purse; she grasped Mabel's hand. "My dear man, do you speak English? Mabel is not going anywhere without me, and that's final."

"Nyet," snapped the Russian officer.

Mabel, gathering courage from Violet, asked, "Nyet, you don't speak English? But you answered, so you do speak English." She would not let this little man intimidate her.

The cherub-faced officer looked menacingly at Mabel. "I speak English," he said in his heavily accented Russian. "But my answer is still nyet. Your friend is not accompanying you. You are coming with me alone, and you are to come now."

"Well then, nyet, right back at you. I am Mabel's spokesperson and a lawyer if you like. No one will question Mabel unless I am with her. Do you understand?"

Mabel looked at her friend with shock and admiration. Violet hated confrontation.

Smirnov looked thoughtfully at the two women who were holding hands. "Fine, fine, come."

Good on Violet, thought Mabel, round one. Maybe together, they could brazen it out.

Smirnov ushered them into a small room behind the lobby desk. Mabel's trepidation returned as she looked around the wood-panelled room. Hanging on the office walls were pictures of men in tuxedos posing on the hotel steps with the Russian president. And a large, framed photo of the president hung on the wall behind a gray metal desk where Inspector Lebedev sat. He stared at Smirnov.

After a brief exchange in Russian, the inspector paused, eyeing the two ladies before him.

Violet squeezed Mabel's hand as they waited for the inspector's response.

"Please, sit down," he requested politely.

Mabel looked apprehensively over her shoulder at Officer Smirnov standing by the door with his feet spread and hands clasped behind his back. Did they think they would make a break for it? Over in a corner by a filing cabinet sat Leon. Her eyes widened. She smiled timidly at him. "Hello, we were wondering where you were?"

"Now you know," he tersely replied.

"Never mind, Mr. Peeters, take a seat," ordered Inspector Lebedev.

What the heck was Leon doing here? Mabel gave the man a worried look and took a seat on a wooden ladder-back chair. Her feet didn't touch the floor. She wiggled forward, sitting on the edge of the chair. Violet pulled up a matching chair and sat beside her. Mabel straightened her shoulders, determined not to let the Russian police officer intimidate her. She'd faced down killers in the past. She could handle a little questioning. But she was glad she was sitting down; it was Russia.

"Your passports, please." The inspector smiled, but his gaze was steely cold.

Violet opened her purse and placed her passport on the desk. She stood looking down at Inspector Lebedev, arms folded across her chest.

"You may sit down."

"Thank you. I will. When you are through inspecting my passport."

Mabel's confidence soared as she watched with admiration at her friend's spunky attitude.

"Your passport appears to be in order," Inspector Lebedev said, handing Violet her passport. "Officer Smirnov has informed me you are this woman's lawyer?"

"You may call me that. I am Mrs. Havelock's representative."

"Why do you think Mrs. Havelock needs a lawyer?" Inspector Lebedev, his forearms resting on the desk, steepled his fingers and stared coldly at Violet.

"Ah, well, ah," sputtered Violet, her spunkiness disappearing. "I'm..., I'm her friend. And, and we like to be together."

Mabel bit her lip; her stomach did flip-flops. Poor Violet. This was all her fault; she'd dragged Violet into this mess. There was a long, awkward pause as Violet and Mabel shifted uneasily in their chairs.

## THE SUSPECTS 223

Finally, Inspector Lebedev's steely gaze fell on Mabel. "I am waiting. Your passport," he demanded.

Mabel's heart leaped; she slid off the chair and set her purse on the desk, pulling out the contents one by one, first wads of Kleenex, hand wipes. Her coin purse, then her wallet. She smiled timidly at the man behind the desk and continued to rummage in her purse. Finally, she dumped the contents onto the desk. "Dear me, what have I done with the silly thing?" She looked fearfully at the officer. What if she lost it? She'd be trapped in Russia forever. It just had to be here somewhere.

Inspector Lebedev's index finger drummed on the desk.

"You have it, Mabel, I know you have," Violet encouraged, twisting the strap of her purse.

"Aha, I knew I had the silly thing somewhere." Unzipping a pocket of her purse, she produced her passport. Her hand shook as she handed it to the inspector.

He scooped it up and read aloud. "Mabel Havelock," he said, mispronouncing her last name.

Mabel stuffed Kleenex and hand wipes back in her purse. She dropped her coin purse on the floor and stooped to pick it up. "Oh, goodness, me." She giggled nervously. "That isn't how you pronounce my name. You're as bad as Hilda. But don't worry. I probably couldn't pronounce your name either. How do you say your name? Is it Libbyoff?"

"I think it's pronounced Ladyoff," Violet suggested.

"Do you think so?"

"My name is neither Libby nor lady, and there is no off," snapped the inspector.

Mabel turned to the officer by the door and smiled proudly. "But I can pronounce your name, Smirnov. Are you related to the Smirnov family, which makes vodka? Their vodka is very famous in my country. Very popular."

The short, round man laughed. "Nyet."

"I think it's a company, dear, not a family," corrected Violet. Her voice was unruffled, but her fingers, twisting her purse strap, belied the calm.

"Well, someone owns the company. And their vodka is excellent, don't you think?" prattled Mabel. Maybe if they played the old lady card, the Russian Police Inspector would dismiss them as two silly old ladies, and they would evade serious questioning about the keycard and desk chair.

"I'm not partial to it, but if you mix it with clamato juice, it's quite nice. Do you have clamato juice in Russia? It's a favourite in Canada, where we come from. We use it with vodka to make a cocktail called a Caesar. Have you heard of it?" babbled Violet.

Mabel bit her lip to hide her grin. Great, Violet was playing along. "Yes, I like a Caesar. But I hate it when they put a sprig of asparagus in it."

"Me too; it should be celery." Violet giggled nervously.

"Vegetables and juice." The inspector raised his voice. "Please stop talking about vegetables. This is a serious matter regarding the death of this tour director."

"Yes, of course, dear," Mabel scrambled back up on her chair. Her stomach churned. Did he know what they did?

When Mabel said '*dear*,' the inspector arched an eyebrow. He inhaled, then blew out a breath. He opened Mabel's passport and said, "This is your passport."

"My dear man, of course, it's my passport; you can tell by the picture. I'm not proud of that picture. Why do they take a picture without glasses? I always wear glasses," Mabel babbled. Maybe she could faint; she was feeling sick, so fainting wouldn't be hard. Then he couldn't question her. But that would leave poor Violet, and she could never abandon Violet. She wished she could come up with a reason for the desk chair and keycard, but no idea came to mind. Damn it, she and Violet should have rehearsed an answer. But dear Violet was such an honest person and such a poor liar. She glanced over at Leon. Was that a smirk on his lips? What did this man know? Did he see them wheel Hilda down the hall? Or was he the killer, hoping to trap them into taking the fall?

"I am not your dear man. And what do you know about the death of this tour director?" asked the inspector.

Mabel felt a burning in her chest; her breathing was erratic; she tried to catch her breath, but her chest tightened. Oh, dear Lord, she was having a heart attack. A heart attack in Russia. She was going to die right here in this room. An irrational thought raced through her mind. What would her kids say?

# Chapter Thirty-One

"Mabel, are you all right?"

Mabel placed a hand on her chest; the pressure was worse. She looked frantically at her friend.

"Oh dear, I think you're having a panic attack." Violet looked wildly around the room. "Is there a paper bag?"

The pressure was building. Mabel leaned forward, gasping.

"A panic attack? Why are you panicking? You have something to confess," accused Inspector Lebedev.

"Bwaaap," Mabel burped. Then, feeling immense relief, she burped a second time. She put her hand over her mouth. "There, I feel better. Ops, please excuse me. Sorry, that wasn't very ladylike."

Violet pulled out a bottle of water from her purse. "Here, have a drink."

Mabel unscrewed the top, taking a big swig.

"Are you quite over your malady?" the inspector asked, a look of distaste on his face.

Mabel wiped her mouth with a tissue and screwed the lid back on the water bottle. "Yes, thank you." She did feel better, nervous, but better.

"Then answer the question," demanded Lebedev.

"What question was that? I forget."

# THE SUSPECTS

"Me too," chipped in Violet.

"You have something to confess."

"That's not a question, dear," Violet corrected.

"My title is Inspector Lebedev, not dear," rebuked the inspector.

There was a snicker from Smirnoff. Which quickly turned into a cough as the inspector glowered at the officer standing by the door.

"Be that as it may, that was not a question," Violet said earnestly.

Inspector Lebedev sighed. "What do you know about Miss Hilda?" He glanced down at a passport sitting beside Mabel's. "Karlson."

"She was, of course, our tour director. We met her in Copenhagen. May I have my passport back?"

"You know nothing about her?"

"No, why would we know anything about Hilda? She's from Denmark. We live in Canada. Can I have my passport back?"

The inspector picked up Mabel's passport and then laid it back down on the desk. "You both were with Annika Nilsson when she discovered Hilda Karlson's dead body."

"Yes, we were." Why wasn't he giving her passport back? He gave Violet hers.

"What did you see?"

"Besides the dead body?"

"Of course, besides the dead woman," thundered Inspector Lebedev.

"Please don't shout; it could bring on my malady." She'd play the old lady card. Maybe gain some sympathy.

"Did you see anyone?"

"Well, no, if the killer was still in the room, they were certainly hiding."

"Maybe under the bed. We didn't look there," Violet volunteered.

"Did you?" asked Mabel.

The inspector frowned. "Did I what?"

"Did you look under the bed?"

"Do not be ridiculous," snapped Inspector Lebedev.

Mabel wasn't sure, but either Smirnov or Leon chuckled.

The inspector's eyes darted around the room, and he took a deep breath and exhaled. "What I meant to say was, did you see anything suspicious, anything out of the ordinary?"

"Besides a dead Hilda?" asked Mabel, her stomach gave another lurch.

The inspector's face took on a red hue.

"The chair, that was odd," Violet interjected.

Mabel's eyes widened, her mouth went dry, she tried to swallow. She twisted the lid off the water bottle, taking a sip. Good Lord. Why was Violet bringing that extra chair to their attention? Was she nuts? Now, they were in for it.

"The chair?"

"Yes, I personally think it's not right that Hilda had two desk chairs in her room, and we don't even have one." Violet lifted her chin and folded her arms, staring boldly at the inspector.

"Maybe Hilda got two because she is a tour director," Mabel said quickly. She bit her lip; that didn't make sense.

"What is Hilda going to do with two chairs?" asked Violet.

## THE SUSPECTS

"Well, nothing now. She is dead," countered Mabel, her mind searching for a better answer. How was she going to divert the Inspector from that darn chair? And darn Violet, what was she thinking?

"Ladies, ladies, would you please get back to the matter at hand? Forget about the furniture."

Mabel felt giddy; they just might get away with the extra chair in Hilda's room. Violet was a genius.

"Easy for you. You aren't staying in this hotel." Violet pursed her lips.

Oh, Violet, Mabel worried. Don't push it.

Violet continued. "Anyway, it's lucky it was handy, as we had to help Annika into the chair. She was having a meltdown."

"Meltdown?"

"Yes, poor girl," lamented Mabel. "I imagine it is her first time seeing a dead body."

"And the dead body of Hilda Karlson did not bother you? Why is that?" asked the inspector, tapping and spinning Mabel's passport.

"Well, of course, it was a shock, but Violet and I are retired nurses. Hilda is not the first dead person we have seen."

"I see." The inspector tapped Mabel's passport with his forefinger.

Mabel cast Violet a worried look. He still wasn't giving her back her passport.

"Oh, and the keycard. The keycard was lying on the floor," Violet said.

Mabel shot Violet a shocked look. They might get away with the chair, but her fingerprints were all over that card.

"The keycard?"

"Yes, on the floor. Unfortunately, dear Mabel is a neat freak." Violet smiled innocently. "Neat freak doesn't mean she is crazy," she added hurriedly. "It means she can't stand things untidy."

"Me?" Mabel's eyes rolled.

"Yes, dear, don't deny it. You know you are." Violet turned back to face the inspector. "Mabel, doing her neat and tidy thing, picked up the card."

Mabel made a silent vow never to underestimate her friend again. "Yes, yes, I must confess I do like things neat and tidy. For instance, the picture of your president is tilted; it's not hanging straight. It's driving me crazy. But not really crazy, you understand?"

The inspector turned to look over his shoulder, then back at Mabel.

"I so want to straighten it."

"Dear, it's not crooked," disputed Violet.

Mabel bit back a smile; Violet couldn't help herself. "Oh, maybe you are right."

"What are you on about? This is a murder investigation. Not good housekeeping," snarled Lebedev. "Back to the murder room."

Violet sat up straight in her chair and pursed her lips. "What an interesting way to describe poor Hilda's—"

"Enough," he shouted.

"Please don't shout; it could bring on Mabel's malady again. We are just trying to explain to you why dear Mabel picked up the keycard. Where did you put it, dear?"

"Gosh," exclaimed Mabel. "I really don't know. I'm sure it's somewhere in the room."

"I wonder if you dropped it in the excitement of finding poor Hilda?"

"Maybe, I can't remember. I could have. It was...." Mabel trailed off.

"Yes, who knows, a lot was happening, and so fast. Finding Hilda dead with a knife in her. And Annika, having her meltdown."

Violet should be on stage, marvelled Mabel.

"Besides the keycard," Inspector Lebedev's eyes narrowed. He tapped the passport. "Did anything else seem odd?"

Mabel gave Violet a sidelong look. A tiny hint of a smile appeared on Violet's lips as she looked down at her hands clasped in her lap. "You mean besides a knife sticking into poor Hilda?" she asked.

The inspector rubbed his forehead, sighed, pushed the passport to the side, folded his hands on the desk, and leaned forward. "Yes," he said slowly, an edge to his voice. "Besides the knife."

Mabel debated whether she should mention the antifreeze. "No, nothing," she said.

"Why did you dislike Hilda Karlson?" Inspector Lebedev barked. Giving Mabel an unrelenting stare.

Mabel gulped. "I never said I disliked Hilda."

"Your friend told us you argued with her every day."

"What friend? Violet, did you say I argued with Hilda?"

"No, dear, I didn't. Inspector, please don't put words in my mouth."

The inspector closed his eyes for a second and exhaled. "Members of your tour group reported that you, Mrs. Havelock, argued with Miss Karlson daily."

"I wouldn't say every day." Mabel squirmed in her seat, recalling her confrontations with the tour director.

"What were the conflicts about?"

"The airline lost my luggage."

"And you blamed Hilda Karlson for this loss."

"No, it was more about her deliberately mispronouncing my name."

"Hum, a bit petty."

"Yes, I thought so; she did it deliberately."

"I mean, you were petty."

"Me, petty?"

"Hilda was a bully. If everything went her way, she was all sweetness and light. But the minute it didn't, she came down on whoever annoyed her like a ton of bricks," defended Violet. "Surely, the other tour members told you that. She even turned on Annika and Bjorn."

Mabel nodded, thinking of Herman. The man was on the receiving end of Hilda's scorn many times. He intimated that he would get even. Should she name him?

"What the other people have said is no concern of yours."

"I beg to differ; they have named me," protested Mabel. "And besides, my baggage was not lost. It was on the bus. I saw it last night when we checked into this hotel. That's why Hilda and I had it out in the lobby."

"Had it out?"

"That's why I was so mad. Hilda and Bjorn, for some crazy reason, hid my luggage on the bus."

"You wanted Hilda Karlson dead. You were angry because you thought the bus driver and Hilda hid your luggage," the inspector said. "You went to her room, and you lost your temper, and you killed Hilda Karlson."

Mabel blanched. The reason he never gave her passport back was because he thought she had killed Hilda.

"Don't be silly. Mabel is hardly going to kill Hilda over a lost suitcase. Even if it was hidden on the bus."

"What do you mean, even if? My poor battered bag was on that bus."

"Well, yes, sorry. I know Bjorn and maybe Hilda hid your suitcase. And even if they did —"

"And maybe Hilda?"

"Dear, you don't know if she did."

"Ladies." Inspector Lebedev drummed his fingers on his desk, giving the ladies an irritated look.

"Yes, I do," Mabel said. "When I confronted Hilda in the lobby last evening, she told Bjorn to bring my suitcase in. She didn't ask if it was on the bus. So, she darn well knew."

"Okay, you're right. But as I was saying, even if they hid your suitcase, there is no way you would—"

"There you go again; it's not even if they hid my suitcase. They did hide it."

"Ladies," interrupted Inspector Lebedev.

"You're getting this wrong, Mabel. Just because they misplaced your suitcase, you wouldn't kill Hilda for a misplaced—"

"Yes, misplaced." It suddenly occurred to Mabel that Violet was trying to clear her. And she was digging a hole for herself.

"Ladies, stop your bickering," demanded Lebedev.

"We're not bickering. We are discussing. We never bicker," contradicted Mabel.

Violet nodded. "No, we never bicker, well there was that one time—"

"Stop, stop," Lebedev thundered, slapping his hand on the desk. Mabel and Violet both jumped, looking at the inspector in surprise.

"You have just revealed that you believe Hilda Karlson was responsible for hiding your baggage. You argued with her. You were angry. You murdered Hilda Karlson." Lebedev leaned forward, his eyes boring into Mabel's. "We have witnesses to what happened."

"Witnesses?" Mabel sucked in her breath; her voice shook. Violet gasped, her face ashen.

Mabel licked her dry lips. They'd been seen taking Hilda's body back to her room. By who? The killer? It didn't matter; her worst fears had just come true. They had moved a dead body, incriminating themselves with the murder. And she had dragged poor Violet down with her.

"We have witnesses who told us you argued with Hilda Karlson. And you uttered threats."

"Threats!" Mabel's mouth dropped open. She almost giggled. So it was just the stupid argument with Hilda. And not about moving the body. Violet gave her hand an encouraging squeeze.

Lebedev gave Mabel a piercing look. "Answer. Did you?"

"Did I what?" Mabel asked, trying to buy time. What had she said to Hilda? She opened the water bottle and took a swig.

"Did you not say." The inspector opened a notebook on the desk and read. "*I will be your worst nightmare. You had better keep looking over your shoulder because I will be there. You'll get yours if it's the last thing I do.*"

"What? When? I, I don't think so." Mabel coughed. Did she really say that? She couldn't remember. Maybe she did. She wiped her mouth with the back of her hand.

"You do not think so? Then I put it to you. That you did. You threatened Hilda Karlson. And now she is dead." Inspector Lebedev's eyes bored into hers. "This keycard you say you found on the floor. We have found this card. And when we take your fingerprints, we will find your prints on it."

"Yes, ... I, we explained." Mabel's heart pounded. The Inspector seemed determined to pin Hilda's murder on her.

"That is a fabrication. You used this card to gain access to Hilda Karlson's room and stabbed this woman in a fit of rage."

"I didn't threaten Hilda," sputtered Mabel. "And, and I didn't kill her."

"You did threaten her. We have several witnesses who said you threatened to kill Hilda Karlson."

"What a load of hogwash," blurted Mabel. She took a deep breath and began to breathe slowly in and out. Wasn't that how you controlled panic?

"Hogwash?"

"She means that the allegations are false," Violet said.

"I will decide what is false." Lebedev slammed the palm of his hand on the desk. Mabel shrunk back in her chair; her heart lurched.

"You were heard issuing threats on more than one occasion. Did you not say I've had it? No more Mrs. Nice Canadian? I'm going to let her have it with both barrels?"

Mabel's eyes narrowed. Herman, that rat. She remembered saying something to that effect. It was after Herman's altercation with Hilda at The Summer Palace. But he'd uttered more threats than she ever thought of. Was he using her to cover his tracks?

"Mabel may have said something like that. But for goodness' sake, Hilda wasn't shot," Violet defended. "And Mabel most certainly didn't kill Hilda."

"There were more threats." He looked down at his notes. "*You better keep an eye out for me. Because I'll get you if that is the last thing I do.*"

"I...I don't think I said it quite like that." Mabel's lips trembled. She was sure she didn't say it like that. Good Lord, she was the prime suspect in the murder of Hilda because of a few ill-chosen words. "I...I just meant I was going to report Hilda to the tour company. And she would pay for hiding my luggage."

"How much?"

"How much what?"

"How much money did you want from her?"

"No, not money. My threats, if they were threats, were about Hilda's job. Not her life."

"*I will get you if it is the last thing I do.* That is a threat in any language. And now the motive is clear. You were going to report Hilda Karlson to the tour company unless she paid you. When she refused to pay you your blackmail money. You became angry. Angry enough to kill her," accused Inspector Lebedev.

# Chapter Thirty-two

Violet jumped off her chair and strode to the desk. She slapped her hands on it, leaned over the desk, and glowered at the inspector. "This is ridiculous. Mabel is hardly going to poison Hilda."

Mabel was astounded. She looked with admiration at Violet. Violet, who hated confrontation, was going to bat for her.

"Poison?"

Violet planted her feet, crossed her arms, and said, "Yes, Hilda was poisoned. Where would Mabel—"

"You, my good woman, are making an absurd statement. Hilda Karlson was found in her bed and stabbed with a knife. You are trying to divert the suspicion from your friend. It won't work."

"Yes, the knife in poor Hilda's chest is a puzzle," Mabel said. "But Hilda was poisoned."

"Poisoned?" Lebedev turned to Leon. The men exchanged a rapid-fire conversation in Russian, with Smirnov joining in.

Mabel watched open-mouthed as the exchange in Russian between the three men continued. Who the heck was Leon? Secret police? Or some kind of Russian spy? And if he was, who was he spying on?

Violet returned to sit next to Mabel. She nudged her with her elbow. "This should put you in the clear. They can't possibly think you carried a can of antifreeze around with you."

As Smirnov tapped on his phone, Lebedev turned and looked first at Violet, then at Mabel. "What are you whispering about?"

"Can we go now? I didn't stab Hilda, and I didn't poison her."

Lebedev gave them a steely look. "Why do you keep saying poison? Explain this ridiculous poison theory of yours."

"It's not a theory." Mabel glanced at Leon. Leon leaned forward, his arms resting on his knees, looking intently at her.

"Not a theory? You saw the knife," Lebedev said. "Your knife."

Mabel tilted her head, looking through her granny glasses at the inspector. "Not my knife, and yes, we certainly did see the knife. Remember, we discovered the body."

The inspector took a deep breath and snarled, "Poisoned! You are trying to blame someone else with this poison story. Poisoned? Your knife was sticking into this woman's chest."

"I repeat, it's not my knife. And Violet and I are positive Hilda was poisoned." Violet nodded in agreement.

"Poisoning? You are familiar with poisoning?" The inspector's steely look was unwavering.

"It doesn't take a genius to smell antifreeze. We are both familiar with that smell. We live in Canada, and antifreeze is used in the winter in the radiators of our cars."

"Antifreeze?"

"Yes, antifreeze."

"You are trying to tell me that someone poisoned Hilda with antifreeze."

"I told you we smelt it," Mabel replied. "It was unmistakable. Surely you detected it?"

"This smell, you are sure you know this antifreeze odour?"

"I know the smell of antifreeze. My car had a radiator leak, and it puddled on my garage floor. It has a very distinctive smell. At first, we thought the green liquid in the bottle on Hilda's night table was crème de menthe. But it wasn't. It was antifreeze."

Lebedev frowned but remained silent; he looked at Smirnov. The cherub officer pocketed his phone and nodded to his superior.

"Antifreeze?" asked Lebedev.

"Da," answered Smirnov, nodding.

The men stared at Mabel and then glanced at each other.

"You just found out? The Moscow police missed a vital piece of evidence?" Mabel asked with a smug look on her face.

"Mabel," cautioned Violet, gripping her friend's arm.

"Ouch." Mabel pulled her arm away.

Violet pressed her lips together in a thin line, shaking her head.

"The Moscow City Police Force is the best police force in the world," stormed the inspector. "You and your friend here are two old—"

"I hope you are not going to say, two old ladies. That would be so rude. We dislike rudeness." Mabel pursed her lips.

Violet shot Mabel a warning look. Now confident she was free of murder allegations, Mabel regained her confidence and lifted her shoulders in a shrug.

"No, of course not. But as you are not a policeman, woman, a person," sputtered Lebedev. He sucked in a deep breath and asked, "How did you identify this antifreeze smell?"

"I told you we live in Canada and use antifreeze in the winter in our vehicles. Do you have trouble remembering things? Perhaps you should take more notes in that little notepad of yours."

Violet pinched Mabel's arm again.

"Ouch." Mabel rubbed her arm.

Lebedev slammed his closed fist on the desk; he stood, and the desk chair flew back, striking the wall. The picture of the Russian president tipped. "Enough of your insolence," he shouted.

Violet flinched, looking at the crooked picture; she pointed. "Oh my, I'm sorry, but—"

"It is your friend who should be sorry," snarled the inspector.

Mabel flinched, but she held his look as he strode around the desk to loom over her.

"No, I'm sorry, but your president is crooked," Violet said meekly.

"What? How dare you?" Inspector Lebedev turned to confront Violet.

"I'm sorry, but you did it. Your president's picture is crooked. I didn't have anything to do with it," Violet's voice quivered as she shrank back in her chair.

The inspector turned and paused to look at the lopsided photo of the president. "You." He motioned to Smirnov. "Fix it."

Smirnov raced over, adjusting the photograph.

## THE SUSPECTS

The inspector waited until satisfied the picture was straight and turned his attention to Mabel. "Well?" he thundered.

Mabel's first instinct was to cower in her chair. Instead, she straightened her shoulders and said haughtily. "Sorry, but I am surprised your forensic team didn't spot the smell immediately. Your vehicles here must use antifreeze in the winter. They should know what it smells like."

Inspector Lebedev folded his arms and leaned back on his desk, staring intently at Mabel. He opened his mouth to speak.

"Mabel, it gets cold in Denmark. They probably use antifreeze," Violet said before the inspector could get a word out.

"Oh my gosh, the bus." Mabel brought a hand up to her mouth. Why had they never thought of Bjorn? It was so obvious. Bjorn, the bus driver, could have antifreeze for the bus. Or he would know where to purchase it. He'd driven this route to Moscow many times.

"You said the bus. Why do you say the bus?" asked Inspector Lebedev.

What should they say? Should they say they thought Bjorn was the killer? What would his motive be? She'd been falsely accused. She'd hate to do that to someone else. "I'm worried I will miss the bus to the Cossack dancing," evaded Mabel.

Leon stood and walked purposely over to stand by Inspector Lebedev and stared accusingly at Mabel. "I don't think you are worried about missing the bus."

"Just who the heck are you?" demanded Mabel.

"I'm an Interpol Agent."

"Aha, I knew there was something fishy about you." Smiling, Mabel folded her arms across her chest.

"Fishy?" asked Inspector Lebedev.

"You know, don't you?" Leon asked, looming over her.

"We know what?"

"You know it was Bjorn."

Mabel looked warily up at him. "You mean, do we suspect him of killing Hilda?"

"Yes."

"Bjorn Hanson, the bus driver?" Lebedev asked, confronting the Interpol Agent.

Leon held up a hand. Lebedev scowled but sat back on the edge of the desk.

Mabel exchanged a look with Violet. The power had shifted from the inspector to Leon. "Well, I expect Bjorn has ready access to antifreeze," Mabel said. "Who else on tour would have antifreeze? But why on earth would he kill Hilda? Was she in cahoots with Bjorn in some nefarious scheme regarding my suitcase? It makes no sense."

"I doubt Hilda Karlson was in cahoots, as you put it. I think she discovered Bjorn was hiding your suitcase, and I suspect she was going to report Bjorn or blackmail him. And he needed to silence her," Leon said.

"I do not think a bus driver would kill to keep his job," scoffed Inspector Lebedev.

Mabel glared at the inspector. He was quite ready to pin the murder on her for a lost suitcase.

Leon turned to face the police officer. "No, not because he would lose his job. To keep from going to prison. I have been on the trail of two international smugglers who deal in stolen antiquities, usually jewellery and small ornaments. They smuggle them out of the country to sell to rich collectors."

"Yes, I have been informed of your investigation by my superiors," Lebedev said; he folded his arms across his chest. "But you have yet to disclose your findings. My superiors and I are waiting."

"I needed proof," Leon replied. "We had a tip that the smugglers were on this tour. My job was to find out who they were and gather enough evidence to arrest them. Our informant didn't know who the contacts were or how they smuggled the stolen items out of the countries. The only thing I was sure of was the smugglers were on this bus tour."

"Did you wear disguises?" asked Mabel.

Leon arched his eyebrows in surprise. "Yes, I did. Very observant."

Mabel wanted to add that he was wearing a wig now. But smiling smugly, she refrained.

"Back to this bus driver," Lebedev said abruptly. He turned, picking up his notepad off the desk, and read, "Bjorn Hanson, a national from Sweden. You suspect him of smuggling?"

"No, he's not a smuggler. Bjorn is the contact. He sets up the meetings between the thieves and the smugglers. And in case they were stopped and searched at customs, they needed to hide the stolen jewellery. That is where your suitcase came in, Mabel. I expect Bjorn intercepted your suitcase when the airline delivered it to the hotel in Copenhagen."

"It was on the bus the whole time?"

"Yes, I believe so."

"Now everything makes sense. When I opened my bag last night, I found my clothes in a jumbled mess. And Violet found a ticket to the museum in Oslo."

"When you demanded your bag last night. Bjorn had to empty it out fast. And in the dark, he missed the Viking Museum ticket," Violet said and added. "Somehow, that ticket dropped into your luggage when they stowed the jewellery."

"That rat had my suitcase the whole time, and if my suitcase was searched by customs, I would have taken the fall for the stolen goods."

"Yes, it was a precaution," Leon said. "Bjorn has probably used this method with other tourists. He drives this route many times during the tourist season."

"So Hilda wasn't a part of this smuggling racket?" Mabel asked. Her thoughts went back to Hilda coming to their room. Maybe Hilda came to tell her that it was Bjorn who hid her suitcase.

"No, I don't think Hilda had anything to do with the smuggling," Leon said.

"We will know more when we question this bus driver, Bjorn. And these smugglers? Who are they?" Lebedev levered himself off the desk.

"Allan and Bridget Hughes."

"I knew it, I knew it," Mabel said excitedly. "Violet and I have suspected there was something fishy about them."

"Fishy?" asked Lebedev.

"You suspected them?" Leon looked skeptical.

"Yes, because of Violet's red hair."

"And my glasses, but of course, my hair is a much nicer shade of red. Not nearly as brassy as Bridget's."

"Hair, glasses? What are you on about?" Leon frowned.

"The Scarf Men," Mabel said.

Leon nodded. "Ah, yes, the Scarf Men."

"Yes, the Scarf Men. Obviously, the Hughes didn't know who they were going to buy the stolen goods from. And the thieves wouldn't know who the buyers were. So, Bjorn must have told the Hughes to look for a man with a red and yellow scarf, and the scarf men were told to look for a tall redhead with blue glasses."

"Well, my hair, as I said, is way nicer. But of course, the scarf men wouldn't know that."

"If I get your drift. You mean Violet was mistaken for Bridget," Leon said.

"Yes, what else have we been talking about? Please try to follow the conversation. My goodness, you're as bad as the Inspector."

Smirnov grinned, but the grin quickly faded as the inspector glared.

"And by the way. If you knew it was the Hughes, why didn't you arrest them?" asked Violet.

"Yes, why didn't you?" echoed Lebedev.

"I wanted the whole network. We have arrested the thieves in each of the countries we visited. Moscow was the last leg. This murder is unfortunate."

"Especially for Hilda," Mabel said.

Leon paused. "Well, yes, of course."

"And this Hilda found out the bus driver Bjorn was part of the smuggling ring, and he killed her to shut her up," concluded the Inspector.

"I bet Bjorn was hoping the antifreeze would go undetected. And Hilda's death would be determined as natural causes," exclaimed Mabel excitedly.

The men swung around to stare at her. "Oh, sorry, I guess you already know that."

"Should I remove these meddling women?" asked Smirnov.

Mabel planted her hands on her hips, looking defiantly at the cherub cop. "Meddling? Who told you about the antifreeze?"

"And we still have the knife," pondered the inspector, ignoring Smirnov. "Why did Bjorn kill Hilda Karlson twice?"

"Well, technically, you can't kill someone twice," Violet interjected.

"Yes, that's true," agreed Mabel. Her thoughts turned to Annika. Maybe she and Bjorn were in it together. Maybe her meltdown was an act.

"I have a theory as to why the knife was plunged into the dead woman," Leon said.

"Why?" asked the Inspector.

"Not only why, but who. The who is either Allan or Bridget. If Hilda knew about Bjorn, she might have known about them. She might have confronted them, threatening to turn them over to the police. One of the Hughes stabbed Hilda, not knowing she was already dead?"

"Well, we will soon find out," Lebedev said confidently.

# Chapter Thirty-Three

Mabel and Violet entered the lounge first, escorted by the inspector, Smirnov and Yahontov, followed by Leon. The tour members gathered in small groups, some helping themselves to the buffet and others seated with drinks.

Fred and Sheila, who were pouring over sales receipts, looked up curiously. Annika stood, took a deep breath, and asked, "How soon will my tour people be free to go?"

Herman prodded his wife in the ribs with his elbow. "In my experience—"

"Shush, for goodness' sake, shush." His wife shifted away from him.

Allan smirked at Herman as he set his drink glass on a coffee table. The rest of the tour members waited silently.

Bjorn, perched on a wide windowsill, eyed the police officers who stood front and center. Mabel and Violet paused, then took a seat beside Herman and Carmilla.

The inspector, ignoring Annika's request, announced, "Bjorn Hanson, you are under arrest for the murder of Hilda Karlson."

Gasps of surprise and murmurs of disbelief filled the room. "Silence, Smirnov, cuff this man."

Bjorn jumped up from the windowsill, bumping into Cindy. She fell to the floor in front of a startled Mr. Patel. Bert cursed as Bjorn leapt over Cindy, dashing toward the door. Verity perched on the arm of the easy chair, watched open-mouthed as Sam levered himself from the armchair. The short, squat man grabbed Bjorn by the arm, body-slamming the young Swede to the floor. He pressed his knee onto his back. Bjorn, the wind knocked out of him, groaned. Smirnov seized the bus driver's arms, twisting Bjorn's hands behind his back; he applied the handcuffs and pulled the man to his feet.

"No, no." Verity leapt to her feet, rushing over to Bjorn, clutching his arm. "Oh, not Bjorn."

Sam's brow furrowed as he looked from Bjorn to his wife. "What the hell?"

Verity faced the police officers. "Release him, please. He didn't do it. It was me. I stabbed Hilda."

Sam and Bjorn both gaped at Verity in surprise. The police Inspector and Leon exchanged astonished looks. There were more shocked gasps from the tour group.

"Don't be stupid," Sam yelled, pulling her back from the police. "Shut up and sit the hell down."

"Good lord," gasped Mabel. "Why on earth did you stab Hilda?"

Verity turned to address her husband. "I made a mistake," she confessed. "I, I became involved with Bjorn. Hilda was going to tell you about our affair."

"Good God. You stupid little ninny, I would only have dumped you. Now you're going to a Russian jail."

Verity began to cry. Mabel scooted over and put her arm around Verity. "Dear, how did you get into Hilda's room?"

"I bribed a maid to let me in. I, I never meant to kill her; you have to believe me. I tried to reason with her. I pleaded, and pleaded, but she just lay there with a smirk on her face. I lost it, and I stabbed her. I'm so sorry," Verity sobbed.

"For God's sake, woman, keep your trap shut," Sam shouted, attempting to go to his wife. Yahontov put a restraining hand on him. He then produced another pair of handcuffs, snapping them on Verity's wrists.

"You heard her, let me go," demanded Bjorn. "Release me. I didn't kill Hilda. Verity just confessed she did it."

Verity's mascara left a black trail as tears streamed down her cheeks. "It was a spur-of-the-moment thing. I didn't plan on killing Hilda. It was an impulse. I'm so sorry, really I am."

"A spur of the moment? I don't think so." Mabel shook her head. "It wasn't an impulse; you brought a knife with you. Where you got it from, I have no idea. But there was no knife in Hilda's room." She looked at Inspector Lebedev. "I mean, there would be no knife in the room."

"I accidentally took a steak knife from supper. It was very sharp. Hilda didn't even make a sound," moaned Verity.

"She wouldn't. Hilda was already dead," Mabel said.

"What? Already dead." Echoed around the room.

Mabel looked at the bus driver. "Yes, Hilda was dead. She was poisoned. Bjorn killed her."

"Bjorn, you did it for me." Verity broke out into louder sobs.

"No, not for you, Verity," Leon interrupted. "Hilda was blackmailing Bjorn. She was going to tell the authorities."

"About what? Because of my silly affair with Verity?" snorted Bjorn. "Don't be ridiculous. Release me."

"Bjorn is a criminal," continued Leon. "He is part of a smuggling ring that smuggles stolen valuables."

Allan and Bridget exchanged worried looks.

"Seriously," Herman said excitedly. "I can't wait to tell the folks back home. They won't believe it."

"Allan Hughes and Bridget Hughes, you are both under arrest for smuggling stolen goods," ordered Leon.

"You have no proof," blustered Allan.

"Your room is being searched. We will have all the proof we need." Lebedev turned to Yahontov. "Cuff them."

"But first, remove their vests. I believe you will find a great deal of money stashed in the pockets of their vests," instructed Leon.

"These are my men," snapped Lebedev. "I am cooperating with you, as instructed by my superiors. But remember whose country you are in."

"Yes, of course, my apologies."

Allan leaped across the coffee table, seizing Mrs. Patel and pulling her up from her seat. He put his arm across her throat. "Stand back. Bridget and I are leaving. Don't try to stop us."

Mr. Patel jumped up, grappling with Allan. Allan shook him off, frog-marching Mrs. Patel toward the door, Bridget following.

"Don't be ridiculous. Leave Mrs. Patel alone," Mabel scolded. "You're a smuggler, not a killer. And just how far do you think you'll get?"

Smirnov pushed Mabel out of the way. The cherub-face officer pulled out his pistol and aimed it at Allan. "I am an expert marksman. I will not miss. The woman, let the woman go."

Allan released Mrs. Patel, and she collapsed into her husband's arms.

The Hughes were stripped of their khaki vests and led away with Bjorn and a weeping Verity.

"Bjorn killed Hilda. This is so hard to believe," exclaimed a white-faced Annika.

"Verity was never the sharpest knife in the drawer," Sam snorted. "Stabbing a dead woman. I wonder what the charges are? I'll call my lawyer," he said as he strode out the door.

"It appears he still has some feelings for her," Violet murmured to Mabel.

Annika rose from the couch, took a deep breath, and said, "I guess I'm in charge. But please do not worry. I promise I will arrange airport limousines for your departure from the hotel to the airport. Before going to your rooms, come and see me at the time of your limousine pick ups. I will be in the lobby. I have to phone the head office." With her phone clasped to her ear, Annika hurried out of the room.

Mr. Patel, with a comforting arm around his wife's shoulder, followed Annika. The remaining tour group members mingled, discussing the events, exchanging email addresses, and saying a final goodbye.

"I wonder if the hotel gift shop is open? I might be able to buy some Russian stacking dolls," Sheila said, picking up her purse.

"You aren't buying another damn thing. And you can darn well carry all your precious souvenirs. Come on, you need to pack all that junk you already have." Fred stomped to the door. Sheila followed, grumbling about Russian dolls.

"I am so ready to go home," muttered Carmilla.

"It's interesting how the Russian criminal system works—"

"Oh, Herman, for once in your life, just shut up. I'm so sick of your BS. You're a professor of an online university, and you don't know diddly squat," she said, marching out of the room. Herman, with a shocked look on his face, meekly followed.

"A nasty way to end our tour. But at least we don't have to tip the bus driver," Mabel said.

"But Annika deserves a big tip," Violet replied.

"For sure, poor girl," agreed Mabel.

Bert, his arm around Cindy, paused beside Mabel and Violet. "Hey, ladies, we're heading to the bar. Do you want to join us for one last nightcap?"

"No thanks, I want to go to our room," declined Mabel. "It's probably an early call for our flight home, and I need to pack my suitcase. It's a mess."

"This time, make sure your tag says Mabel Havelock," Violet teased.

The End

# About the Author

Besides being an author, Joan Havelange is an accomplished actor, and director of community theatre, which lends well to her writing. She is a world traveller and an enthusiastic golfer.

She lives in a beautiful little town in the middle of the Canadian prairies. A ski hill, lakes, and rivers are just a short drive away. Joan has been writing fiction since her early twenties, beginning with romance stories. She found that she would rather kill them than kiss them and turned to mysteries and never looked back. She is the author of five whodunit mysteries, one thriller, and her latest, a historical mystery.

# Don't miss out!

Visit the website below and you can sign up to receive emails whenever Joan Havelange publishes a new book. There's no charge and no obligation.

https://books2read.com/r/B-A-CCKUC-XWWOF

**BOOKS 2 READ**

Connecting independent readers to independent writers.

Did you love *The Suspects*? Then you should read *The Trouble with Funerals*[1] by Joan Havelange!

*A Mabel and Violet Mystery*
**The Trouble with Funerals**

*How can Mabel solve a murder when her prime suspect has the perfect alibi?*

**JOAN HAVELANGE** [2]

Something nefarious is going on at Gravenhurst Manor. Mabel's mother, Sophie, is positive her best friend, Mini, did not die of natural causes. She convinces Mabel to investigate the suspicious circumstances of Mini's death.

Is there a cold, calculating murder at work? If so, Mabel needs to find the killer before it's too late; her mother could be the next victim.

The trouble is Mabel's main suspect has the perfect alibi, namely Mabel. But why would anyone want to kill a senior?

---

1. https://books2read.com/u/4APpDp

2. https://books2read.com/u/4APpDp

Too bad Mabel's valued sidekick, Violet, is no longer reliable. Violet has gotten herself involved with a man, and Mabel doesn't trust him.

# Also by Joan Havelange

**Mabel and Violet Mysteries**
Wayward Shot
Death and Denial
The Trouble with Funerals
The Suspects

www.ingramcontent.com/pod-product-compliance
Ingram Content Group UK Ltd.
Pitfield, Milton Keynes, MK11 3LW, UK
UKHW040732200225
455358UK00001B/9